Juliet Bravo one

Together with her hus ... e author of well over a hund ... and literary studies to bestselli ... nd produced hundreds of scripts f ... n-word recordings together with ... sm. Recent undertakings have been the ... *airs* and *The Duchess of Duke Street* series of novels

Mollie Hardwick's own works als ... clude *Emma, Lady Hamilton*, *Beauty's Daughter* (Elizabeth Goudge Award for best historical romantic novel of 1976), *Charlie is my Darling*, *Thomas and Sarah*, *Lovers Meeting*, *Willowwood*. and her North Country trilogy, *The Atkinson Heritage*, *Sisters in Love* and *Dove's Nest*.

Mollie Hardwick was born in Lancashire and now lives with her husband in Highgate Village, North London. The *Juliet Bravo* stories are her first books for Pan.

Mollie Hardwick

Juliet Bravo one

'Juliet Bravo' is the call sign given by Headquarters to Inspector Jean Darblay

Pan Original
Pan Books London and Sydney

First published 1980 by Pan Books Ltd,
Cavaye Place, London SW10 9PG
2nd printing 1980

ISBN 0 330 26299 8
Made and printed in Great Britain by
Hazell Watson & Viney Ltd, Aylesbury, Bucks

chapter one

The couple glanced up at the *House for Sale* notice before opening the wooden gate and entering the front garden. Jean noticed with approval that it was small and manageable, a bit overgrown now, in late summer, but nothing Tom couldn't cope with himself. She liked the look of the house, too. Nothing remarkable, just an ordinary semi built in the post-war years, three down and four up, the usual gables, front bay window, small porch, lattice gate round to the back garden.

But its blank windows had a welcoming look. A fanciful person might have thought of them as eyes looking wistfully for a buyer who would be kind to the house and make it feel like a home again. Jean Darblay was not fanciful, but she knew what she liked when she saw it, and was capable of making her mind up on the spot, even about such a large and important thing as buying a house. Tom, stealing a glance at her bright, interested face, knew that she was on her way to a decision even before they left the downstairs rooms – drawing-room, dining-room, decent-sized if old-fashioned kitchen with a service-hatch through.

Good, Jean was thinking. No time-wasting passages or useless steps, such as they had in their present Victorian house. The rooms wanted some redecoration, walls showing the shape of departed furniture and pictures, yellowing once-white paint. But the dining-room was not too bad – livable with for the moment, especially for people who didn't do a lot of formal dining – a late meal on the kitchen table was more the Darblay style, Jean reflected with amusement.

'Well? What do you think?' she asked Tom.

It was quite obvious to him what *she* thought. 'Needs money spending on it,' he replied guardedly, receiving a look of comical disgust in return.

'You've no imagination at all, Tom Darblay.'

'Oh, I've got imagination, love. It's money I lack.' But he was looking round approvingly at the room they were in, the master bedroom with its wide window giving a view over to the moors, misty in the morning light. On a clear day there would be a glimpse of Yorkshire beyond. The suburban avenue lay outside the town of Hartley; there was a pleasant feeling about it. He went to the window. Neighbouring back gardens were tidy. Neatly pruned rose-trees, cropped lawns with an occasional discreet vegetable patch, bird-tables with pointed thatched roofs. Jean liked things to be decent. She saw enough of the other thing down the nick.

He opened a casement window and sniffed the air, scented with grass-cuttings. 'This is us, isn't it,' he said.

'*I* think so.' She wandered into the bathroom, nicely appointed, nothing drastic needed. Tom had paused at a small bedroom, the sort designed by the architect for a child. The Darblays had no children. Tom minded about that; Jean had been told she could never have any. 'This could be my dark room,' he said. Photography was his pet hobby – natural beauty, townscape, human character studies – he was versatile. The only person whose essence he could never capture was his mercurial wife.

'Could we talk about a guest room before a dark room?' Jean inquired.

'What guests is that, then? Your Dad, if we could ever get him away from his golf course? Jean, you're mad, love. I've got virtually nothing in the bank; £4,285 in the building soc., and £450 for the Mini, if we sell it and you take my 1100. That's it, except for my unemployment benefit.'

Tom tried not to sound bitter. Four months before he had been a design engineer at the British Leyland plant at Speke. Then, long doomed, it had closed, and Tom had found himself on the dole, as it had been called in his father's day. Calling it Social Security was all very well, it didn't make the reality any more palatable. Apart from the money loss, he had been dedicated to engineering, though not in the way Jean was dedicated to her twenty-four-hours-a-day job. It had meant a lot to him, and now it was gone, and he was having to watch his wife being the family breadwinner. There were no jobs of his kind to be had around Hartley. If they moved nearer Manchester the story might be different, but they couldn't possibly move with Jean only a fortnight into her new appointment.

She knew that he was worrying again, and turned to him. 'You've got an interview this afternoon, haven't you? Well, don't take a job because you're panicked about not having one.'

He smiled. 'Buy a house instead?'

'Not a house. *This* house. Subject to survey, I want it, Tom. You do, too, don't you? Well?'

'I've never bought a house at a quarter to nine in the morning,' he hedged, but Jean was implacable.

'Are we going to have it – yes or no? I mean, what the hell's £24,000 in this day and age? We've looked at seven houses now.'

Tom shrugged cheerfully. 'Okay. Settled. Get on, now – you've got your work to go to.' But he still sounded unconvinced.

'This house is £2,000 underpriced,' she urged. 'That's worth being a quarter of an hour late at work. And I was promised if we meet the price we won't be gazumped.'

He laughed. 'Gazumped? D'you know how many unemployed there are around here? D'you know how many houses up for sale?'

'This one,' she said, 'concentrate on this one.'

Tom looked down at his wife. He had not too far to look down; she was two inches above police regulation height, five feet six, a match for his tallness. Nobody would be bold enough to call her pretty, but Tom knew that she could be quite beautiful at times, when her strong lively features were lit by her smile. Her eyes were bright with life and awareness, her complexion fresh enough to take care of itself with the minimum of make-up, her hair crisp and short, cut simply and well by herself, for the two hours a week spent by most women on their shampoos and sets was outside Jean's programme. No hairdresser likes to have to take a client out of rollers, half-cooked, because an urgent police call has come through. Her body was slim and strong, slender-waisted and square-shouldered in her dark uniform, covered now by a coat, the peaked cap left in her car. She was thirty-five years old.

She was searching Tom's eyes. It mattered what he felt, even though she knew what she wanted. 'It's almost in Hartley, not nine miles out, as we are now. It'll make things easier for me.'

'Okay, Jean,' he said. 'If you really want it.'

She kissed him for thanks, and was off, running down the uncarpeted stairs and out of the house. He followed slowly, locking up, looking back at the house which was to be theirs, then returning to his Austin 1100. His would be an empty day; just an interview in the afternoon. But Jean's day would be full.

The police station was in the old part of Hartley, a long, ugly Victorian building in what was still largely a Victorian town, now run sadly to seed since the days when its clustering mill-chimneys had symbolized industrial prosperity, a black badge on Lancashire's coat. The town in the valley still had its mills, but they were empty and derelict, a few put to mean uses such as the reprocessing of rags, the rest as dead as Pompeii, the haunts of vagrants and wandering cats. The rows of terraced cottages that had been built for mill-workers housed all sorts now. West Indians, with restless frustrated youngsters, Asians puzzled and fretted by western rules, pensioners living from hand to mouth, young folk fettered by hire-purchase. The streets they lived in, once prosperous and respectable, had come down in the world. The walls were smoke-grimed with the smoke of more than a century, from chimneys which sent it out no more; the Clean Air Act seemed to have passed Hartley by. Because this was Lancashire, where folks were houseproud (it used to be said that housewives there went out of a morning to metal-polish the tramlines), most of the cramped terrace cottages were well-kept, steps and window-sills whitely scrubbed, paint renewed by any man who could be persuaded up a ladder. In their windows dusty plastic flowers sat, jammed into cut-glass vases, or ornamental relics from past days were framed in draped lace curtains – a pottery swan, a plaster Alsatian, the effigy of an Italian child holding up a bunch of cherries.

The public buildings of Hartley had suffered more than the houses. The Town Hall, once the emblem of civic pride, had given over its dome and the capitals of its Corinthian pillars to the local pigeons which, blackened as itself, roosted day and night in its crannies. The few Anglican churches were derelict and vandalized, the Nonconformist chapels brightened only by large paper stickers pasted across noticeboards: *Sunday Evening, 7 p.m. Brother E. N. Fish will speak on What God Wants For Us.* In Hartley's cinemas, Odeon and Capitol and Electric Palace, the lights had long gone out and the stars' faces been peeled from the hoardings. Then Bingo had come, and now that too was gone, to be replaced by emptiness. In the 1950s an enterprising man from London had opened a Little Theatre, putting on at first his own choice of fringe plays, then a rapid succession of box-office hits; the enterprise had ended in bankruptcy. There were people nearby who might be supposed to want culture – the suburbanites, in the leafy district where the Darblays would live, the rich in their great stone houses in the moorland country outside Hartley, the people who rushed up and down the M6 motorway, a few miles distant, or flew in and out of the airport. But they didn't come into Hartley to get it. The only person who had made any sort of profit out of Hartley's aesthetic possibilities in recent years had been an artist who had held a highly successful exhibition in Bond Street based on Hartley's natural element, rain; cramped streets on wet days, a greasy gloss on the cobbles and narrow pavements, a dull shine on grey slate roofs, the fading colours of pop group posters on boarded-up shops, peeling off with damp, faint football slogans scrawled on decaying walls. It was Lowry, critics said, without the matchstick people, and the pictures sold well.

Hartley might have died completely but for the enterprise of its town council in pre-war years – a far-sighted council alarmed by the closure of the mills which were the town's bread-and-butter. One day, they knew, the mills would be finished. Something must take their place – new, viable industry, labour-intensive industry with a low capital investment.

They were clever, or lucky. A big electrics firm moved into the area, and near the factory sprang up an industrial estate. Other, smaller industries followed, injecting a thin life-blood into the depleted veins of Hartley.

There was one such at the back of the police station. Jean drove her Mini into the private car park adjoining it, carefully locking it, for her personal radio was inside. The station building greeted her with a cleaner face than it had shown when she'd taken up her appointment a fortnight before. Her sharp eyes had not been tolerant of the well-established grime and mild squalor which had been good enough for her male predecessor. She had sent in a squad of cleaners to attack the Victorian building and transform it. Now the walls of the narrow corridors had been washed from floor to ceiling, the paintwork scrubbed, the brass doorknobs polished until they glittered. Those who were not in favour of Jean's appointment (and there were not a few) muttered, 'Women!' But there was no denying that the old place looked better.

As she entered her own small, austerely furnished office, Jean automatically switched from her private self to her public one. Other women would still have been in a whirl of excitement about the new house, mentally furnishing and decorating it. To Jean, the shutting of her office door sealed the house off in another world. Here she was Inspector Darblay, in charge of this Section of the Lancashire Constabulary, with forty-three men under her command and twenty thousand people in the area covered by her Section. Her promotion was queried, resented in that formerly male-dominated society. Yet she had reached her post fairly, by seniority and without graft. It was the biggest challenge of her life, her goal since she had joined the police force in her early twenties, and she was determined to succeed in it.

Not without difficulties. She must neither be a sex symbol nor a martinet, friendly and approachable without allowing familiarities. It was not the way the older men of the Section thought of women.

The young were easier. Police Constable Roland Bentley, nineteen and puppyishly eager, gave no trouble at all. And Sergeant George Parrish, though older than Jean herself, accepted her presence placidly enough. He presented himself in her office, his morning snack – a bacon butty – in hand.

'Morning, Inspector.'

Jean looked up. 'Morning, George.'

'The Soroptimists phoned. They says the best day for your lecture would be the sixteenth, and would you confirm.'

She glanced at her heavily ringed calendar. 'Right, George.'

'And – ma'am – is it right you want parade, nine-thirty?'

'Sharp.'

'I'll shout the word.' He departed, giving place to Sergeant Joseph Beck, the senior of Jean's four sergeants. An authoritarian, bluff and brusque, he didn't try too hard to conceal the fact that he thoroughly disapproved of being under the rule of a female. If he behaved sufficiently casually, perhaps she would go away like a bad dream.

'Morning, boss.' It was not a form of address Jean liked, and she would axe it one day. But not yet. He towered over her.

'Morning Joseph.'

'I've brought you the Houseman file. And a customer outside awaits a private word.' It sounded like mockery.

'Aye.' Jean talked, at the right moments, like the northern lass she was. It came naturally, and helped her relationship with men who would have resented a posh accent.

Beck turned at the door. 'What's this about a parade at nine-thirty?'

She met his eyes levelly. 'There's a parade at nine-thirty.'

'We'll be hard put to it to muster five,' he grumbled.

'Five will do.' She had opened the file and was reading it, carefully not noticing the veiled insolence of his half-shrug.

The 'customer' awaiting Jean's leisure was old Ted Watson, well known to the Hartley police as a snout. Ted was getting impatient.

'You said new Inspector would be here at nine,' he complained to Parrish. 'It's twelve past nine on me digital.'

'Inspector Darblay's here,' Parrish assured him. 'Just give her five minutes to put on her face.' Parrish grinned inwardly as he said it.

Old Watson looked shocked. 'What d'you mean, *put on her face*?'

'Make up,' explained the sergeant patiently, with enjoyment. 'The Inspector that's replaced Mr Denton is a lady, Ted.'

'A lady! A bloody woman? I don't believe it.'

'Then you're almost as surprised as we are,' Beck said incautiously, for at that moment Jean's head appeared round her office door. If she heard, she gave no sign. 'Sergeant Beck,' she said, 'get me the papers on Tatman and Fielding.'

'Yes, boss. Oh, Ma'am, this gentleman here, Mr Ted Watson, who's been a very useful informant to us over the years, says he's got some information for us.'

Jean looked Watson up and down. 'What's that, then?' she asked him.

'I've just witnessed a rape, Mrs Inspector,' he said importantly.

'Come in, Mr Watson. Sit down. What d'you mean, you've witnessed a rape? We haven't heard of a rape, have we, Sergeant Beck?'

Before Beck could answer, Watson inquired, 'What's your name, missis?'

'Inspector Darblay.'

'You've took over from Mr Denton? A woman's a bit of a bloody surprise.'

Jean had already learned to ignore this sort of thing. 'What information do you have, Mr Watson?' she asked coldly.

The old man looked sly. 'I want five pound for it. Mr Denton always give me five pound.'

As though she had not heard, Jean said, 'Now just tell me what you've seen.'

Watson launched into a rambling, heavily dramatized account of screams in a copse on Tomey Moor, a girl's cries that she'd been raped by somebody called Peter. Pressed for more details, he asked, 'Do I get me five pound? Then I'll give you a statement.'

Without answering, Jean picked up her telephone and spoke into it.

'Sergeant Parrish, whenever the Super comes in, show him in straight away . . . Now, Mr Watson. I don't know or care what arrangement you had with my predecessor, but I don't drop fivers, ever. If, in future, you have information about any criminal act, you inform us.'

He was prepared to be truculent. 'Oh, bloody do I?'

'Yes, you do.' Protesting loudly, Watson was escorted into the interview room, just as Sub-Divisional Superintendent Lake was being shown into Jean's office. He watched the retreating figure of the old man with amusement.

'Local colour, is he?'

'I think so. I don't know him. Sit down, sir. Social call?'

'Just dropping by. Thought I'd see how you are.' He took out his pipe and slowly lit it, a manoeuvre giving him the opportunity to take in Jean and her surroundings. When it was going nicely he asked, knowing the answer, 'You've been here a fortnight?'

'Exactly fourteen days.'

'I hear HQ have changed the Section's call-sign from Victor Bravo to Juliet Bravo in your honour.'

'That's right, sir.'

He puffed. 'How are the lot taking it – a woman in charge?'

'They're taking their time,' she answered levelly.

'Oh, yes? Worried?'

'No.'

'Where's the main problem?'

'I can handle it, sir. Sergeant Beck – he takes orders with a certain . . . circumspection.'

'Aye. He misses his ales with Mr Denton. They were close for many years, you know. I suppose Beck expected some promotion out of that. No promotion, and he gets lumbered with you.' He met her gaze. 'You need him.'

'I know that, sir. It'll be fine.'

'Drink a few ales with him,' Lake advised. 'Yours is an important appointment, Jean. You're one of the very few women in England running a whole town like this. Our ladies are usually hived off to Juvenile Bureau, Community Services, HQ Training. You're a one-off for this constabulary. And there'll be a few around who'd be pleased if you failed in any way. This is still the unliberated North – men are men, and they're at pains to tell you so.'

'I grew up with that, sir.' She thought of her father, the most considered person in the household, and her three brothers. She had had to fight for equality with them, be more aggressive than ordinary girls, and they had resisted her all the way. It had been a hard slow battle but useful experience. She went on, 'I'm grateful for your advice over the years, and your efforts on my behalf. What about tea, sir?' A cosy, predictable feminine line. But she would not be getting the tea – that was Bentley's job.

'No, I'm just here for a nod. I'm off to see CID in Manchester – oh, and I want a look at the new billiard table.'

She got to her feet, as he did. 'Not new. Just reclothed.'

'Will it make your team play any better?'

Jean smiled. 'I'll put ten pence on it.'

'Next match against our lot?'

'Yes, sir.'

Lake was at the door. 'You're on. Call me if you need help, advice, anything, any time, twenty-four hours a day. Oh, and regards to your husband.'

'Thank you, sir.'

He smiled and was gone. Jean settled down to the business of the morning: the lecturing of the five men on parade about carelessness with personal radio handsets, the investigation of Ted Watson's report of a rape. It took her out to a maisonette where a mother insistently denied that there could be anything amiss with her daughter, in spite of the fact that the girl had not turned up at work that day. The girl's father, pursued to the factory floor, declared that he had nowt to say and that the police were wasting their time.

Jean sighed. It was going to be one of those days, she felt. Then the call came through from Sergeant Parrish.

'It's a Mrs Maskell. About her husband. She's in a state.'

chapter two

The door of the terraced house in the narrow street shook as Rodney Maskell hammered on it with the knocker.

In the kitchen, his wife Madge put down the knife with which she had been peeling potatoes, and turned a worried face towards her daughter, a pale young girl of fourteen who was finishing breakfast.

'Maureen! it's your da. Hide!'

Maureen left the table and scuttled out. She was used to situations of stress between her nervous Irish mother and her violent father. Hiding, she heard the knocker banged again, then the door opening, and her father's voice.

'I've come for her.'

'You just get out of here.' Madge Maskell's voice was trembling, for all her defiant words. 'Go away, I'm calling the police.'

'She's coming wi' me. I'm taking her.'

'No!' Madge slammed the door in his face, then ran in and told Maureen to pack – they were going away, at once. 'All you need for the whole weekend. Toothpaste, toothbrush, homework. Oh, my God, the washing.' She ran out of the back door and began to unpin sheets, pillowcases, underclothes from the clothesline, not noticing the approach of her husband from the house, the weeping Maureen at his side. He had had a key, after all. He carried a twelve-bore shotgun, pointed now at Madge's head.

'I'm going to kill you,' he said expressionlessly. Maureen clutched at him.

'Don't, Da, don't . . . don't, Da!' she shrieked, as her mother fell to her knees on the wet grass, praying.

'Hail, Mary, full of grace, the Lord is with thee. Blessed art thou among women and blessed is the fruit of thy womb, Jesus. Holy Mary, Mother of God, pray for us sinners now and at the hour of our death, Amen . . .'

Maskell had come nearer to her. 'The only reason why I will keep this gun with me is for you,' he said flatly. 'If you tell police I have this gun they'll come after me. If that happens, I will find you wherever you are, and kill you.' He pressed the tip of the gun against the cowering woman's throat, while Maureen sobbed and pleaded with him. Then he turned, raised the gun, and fired at the centre of a sheet hanging on the clothesline, blasting a hole in it. As the explosion died away Madge began to weep, her head in her hands. She didn't see her husband leave, clutching Maureen by the hand.

Jean's expression was grim as she drove towards Hartley Park. It was not her idea of correct police procedure to interview witnesses in public places, but the call from Parrish had sounded urgent.

Hartley Park was a desolate open space donated to the town by some benevolent dead-and-gone councillor, a place of dead-looking trees and bushes, vandalized benches and lamp-standards, flocking pigeons and blackish sparrows. On this damp morning it was not attractive to the layabouts and young mothers with children who were its usual population. Sergeant Beck was immediately visible, sitting on a bench near the entrance, a woman beside him. He anticipated Jean's first question, not angry but not commendatory either.

'What are you doing here?'

He indicated Madge Maskell. 'She wouldn't come to station. This is her statement.'

Madge looked dumbly on as Jean read the official form he handed to her. Then, sitting down, she said, 'Mrs Maskell, you say your husband's taken your child away. You say it was against your will and the child's will. How did he manage that?'

The woman's face was blank, secretive. 'I don't understand you.'

'Well,' Jean persisted, 'if your child didn't want to go off with him, did he use force?'

'Use force?' Beck listened interestedly. He could have told her this was going to be an awkward witness.

'Use force,' Jean repeated patiently. 'Threaten you with violence, a weapon, knife, hammer . . .'

Madge Maskell was carefully not meeting her eye; she was no actress.

'No, he didn't,' she said. 'But he said he – he'd be very angry if I didn't let him have Maureen.' She looked away, conscious of her own failure to convince. She would not have taken a child in, let alone an Inspector of Police.

'Well,' Jean said briskly, 'there's not a lot we can do. No use of force – it's hard to establish that a father has *abducted* his daughter. I'll put a description out to our men, and see if we can pick him and Maureen up. Then you'll have to come into the station and we'll sort things out. You say he made no threats whatever?'

Looking down at her feet, Madge Maskell said, 'No . . .'

'Okay, Mrs Maskell. Next time, we can't take your complaints in a park; you'll have to come down to the station. Come on, Sergeant.'

They left her there, looking forlornly after them.

The two the police would be looking for were at that moment in Maskell's car. Maureen's face was streaked with tears.

'You'll be all right when you've seen this doctor,' her father told her. 'He'll make you better.'

'I *am* all right, Da.'

'You know you're not,' he said roughly. 'Now listen – whatever you do, don't leave me. Don't try to get help. Don't phone the police. If you do, I'll kill your mother.'

The doctor in private practice to whom he drove his daughter was puzzled by the truculent man and the shrinking patient. After examining her, he took her back to the room where Maskell waited.

'What brought you to me?' he asked him curiously, as the girl fastened her blouse and put on her coat.

'I don't believe in the National Health,' Maskell threw at him. 'I don't believe they cure anyone of anything.'

'Oh, come now, Mr Maskell. And that's not what I meant.'

'You've not seen my daughter ill, have you? When she's had her migraines so bad she faints dead away. And God, I wonder sometimes if she's going to die of it!'

The doctor was rapidly forming the opinion that the father, not the daughter, was in need of medical attention.

'I've just given her a quick check-up,' he said. 'She seems reasonably healthy.'

'She's not,' Maskell snapped.

'Is there a stressful situation at home?' Silly question, thought the doctor to himself, when the home contained a man like this one. 'Your daughter tells me you blame her mother for her illness.'

'I do.'

'Why?'

'She'll not get the proper help for Maureen. She takes her down Doctor Herrick. Saving your profession, he's a bloody useless doctor.'

'I don't know a Doctor Herrick. Why do you say he's useless?'

'There's a surgery queue a mile long. He gives her a quarter of a bloody minute and a prescription for nowt more'n aspirin. If you want a proper job done in this country now, you've got to pay for it, like I'm paying you.'

Still prepared to be reasonable, the doctor began, 'That's not necessarily true . . .'

'Don't argue with me! It *is* true.'

'Look – migraine in a fourteen-year-old child can be due to many causes. The main ones are stress, or hormonal imbalance. Your daughter will have to go through a series of tests to establish possible causes. I'll get my secretary to arrange an appointment for her at County General.'

An angry flush mounted to Maskell's face. 'Hey, you wait a minute. Are you telling me I've come all this way here and I'm to pay you money for private doctoring only to get sent down to County General, which I could've got for free off Doctor Herrick? I wasn't born bloody yesterday, you know! You'd better bloody watch it.'

The doctor's reply was incisive. 'Get out of here.'

Maskell jumped to his feet, caught Maureen's hand and

strode out of the surgery, dragging her behind him, his face livid with fury. Hearing them leave, the doctor's secretary brought in a note Maureen had managed to scribble. As the doctor was reading it, a noise outside drew him to the window. In the road, Maskell was savagely smashing a heavy lump of stone through the windscreen of the Jaguar that bore the notice 'Doctor on Call'. Then he got back in his own Cortina, Maureen by his side, and drove away.

Within minutes the note was in the hands of the police, and Madge Maskell was down at the station, making a statement, her resistance broken down by the words her daughter had written: *My Da will kill her. Tell my Mam not to try to get me back or he will kill her. Not to go to police. I am alright.*

'So,' said Jean. 'You think your husband would try to attack you – try to kill you?'

'Yes,' the woman answered shakily. 'You see, it's been boiling up – his rage. Now it's come to a head I know he's going to do something violent to me or Maureen.'

'Go on.'

'When he lost his job, that was what turned him. He was always difficult, like there was a great anger in him – always. But from fourteen months ago, when he got paid off, he got worse. It was mainly the money. He'd been earning a hundred, hundred and fifty a week. Then suddenly, the dole, £31.65. That's all he got. He couldn't cope.'

Jean's gaze was full of understanding. She knew what it was to have a husband suddenly thrown out of a good job and forced on to the dole. But Tom, thank God, was not a Maskell. 'Tell me about Maureen's illness,' she said.

'She'd always had migraines, since she was a kid of seven. Lately they've been terrible. He blamed me, blamed our doctor. It's true he's no good, the doctor, no good whatever. But Rodney feels Maureen is very ill. She *is* ill, but not that seriously. It's him who's really ill.'

Jean was making notes. 'Now, who are his friends, love?'

The woman shook her head. 'No one. He's no friends. He knows it. He said once, his life was like John the Baptist in the desert. It is.'

'If he has no friends, you're the only one who'd have a clue where he might go. We've got to find your husband, Mrs Maskell. You'll have to tell me where to start looking.'

Madge twisted her hands in her lap. 'I don't know. You see, he's cunning. No, it's worse – sick in the mind. I know he's going to harm her.'

'Did he ever undergo any treatment?'

'For being batty? No, it really didn't come to the surface till he lost his job at JAC's.'

Jean was looking thoughtful. 'JAC's washing machines. A huge factory, and empty. That's one place he'd know every square inch of . . .'

Half an hour later Jean and Detective Sergeant Melchett, driven by Beck, were in front of the empty factory building. She called out to the caretaker who had opened the gates for them.

'I'd like to check some of these buildings. You stay here with the sergeant. Just give me the keys. Have you seen the ex-foreman of this plant, Rodney Maskell, around here?'

No, he hadn't, he said, protesting rather too vehemently, thought Jean. Melchett went round to the rear while Jean moved on through the main assembly. In the old paint shop she stopped, alerted by sounds of movement. Round a corner she saw Maskell at the top of some stairs, drinking from a beer can. On a bench beside him was a coffee pot, more cans of beer, and some food. Maureen was there, looking cowed and nervous. A migraine type, thin and anxious like her mother. Maskell had a gun. He was calling down to the caretaker: so the man had known he was here. It was time to get help.

Jean moved silently along the wall. Maskell was upstairs. She could reach Melchett, with care and luck. She pulled up sharply at a voice behind her.

'Understand what this could do to you, love?'

'This' was his gun, pointing at Jean's back. Somehow he had known she was there, and had slipped down another way to the floor she was on. She turned and faced him, saying levelly, 'Put that away.'

'Turn around,' he ordered her. 'Walk. Turn round.'

Maureen was there, half-way down the stairs, pleading with him, begging him not to shoot, but he went on urging Jean in front of him, and calling the girl down. Jean said, very calmly, 'I've got two other police officers outside.'

'And you'll tell 'em – if they make any cheeky moves, you're the one that's for it,' he barked. She knew the tone of his voice, the voice of a man already past the point of no return to sanity. They moved out into the open, Jean and the gunman, the girl tagging miserably behind, until they came into full view of Melchett and Beck, who froze in their tracks. Maskell took the gun away from the small of Jean's back and fired at the nearside tyre of the parked squad car, then, waving at Jean to stay where she was, led Maureen to his own Cortina, got in, and drove away. They had lost him again.

In the station interview room, Madge Maskell was facing Jean.

'Now we don't have a lot of time, Mrs Maskell. Did you know your husband has a shotgun?'

'Yes.'

'Why didn't you tell me about it?'

Madge looked up, her eyes red-rimmed. 'Don't you understand? He said to me – if I told you he had a gun you'd go after him, and if that happened, then he'd find me wherever I was and shoot me.'

Jean kept her temper, with difficulty. 'D'you have any other information that you're keeping back from us? Do you know it's an offence not to have given us that information? Do you realize how serious this is? Think again. Isn't there a single person he'd turn to in trouble – a relative, or a mate? No? Well, think about places. Some place in the years you've lived here, that he'd go, a place to conceal himself and Maureen? Where have you lived in the last ten years?'

Madge said dully, 'First, council flat, Casimir Road. Then, cottage at Elfield.'

'When did you leave Elfield?'

'Two years back. Now I know he was right about it. It's only a half-mile out, but it's like the country. It was a big sprawling cottage, all old and ugly. But he loved it – I didn't. Three years, we were there. I couldn't clean it. No proper kitchen. Always some loose roof slates. I said, "We have to go modern. I can't take this." The day we sold it everything became difficult between us. I was only thinking lately, would he change back to a better man if we went back to the cottage? I saw a notice on it – it's up for sale again.'

She had given Jean the clue . . .

Marly Cottage was just as old and rambling and dilapidated as Madge had said. Jean, Beck and Melchett looked at it through the windows of their Escort, parked near the ramshackle front gate. Beck was for waiting for reinforcements, but Jean got out of the car and advanced along the overgrown path, the two men following. There was no sign of occupation at the front of the cottage. But at the back, parked beside a derelict greenhouse, was the Cortina. They had barely taken in its presence before an explosion shattered the remaining panes of the greenhouse, and the whole structure fell in like an ancient corpse exposed to the air. At a top-floor window was Maskell, behind his twelve-bore. As they dropped flat and began to crawl to cover he shouted, 'I'll kill you! I'll kill anyone who comes for her!'

In the lane outside the garden Jean ran to the Escort and spoke into her personal radio. 'Inspector Darblay here . . . Marly Cottage, Mill Water Lane. Rodney Maskell, fifty-one Burton Road, Hartley, discharged shotgun at me. I want firearms and sniper here. And please put radio on "talk-through". Over.'

The mobiles arrived first, parking quietly out of range of the cottage windows. A dog-handler and his Alsatians merged into the shadow of some trees. Two Firearms Officers, carrying hand-guns, moved to strategic positions. Jean radioed to Superintendent Lake, at the station.

'How is it?' he asked.

'Serious. He's in this cottage with his daughter and a twelve-bore. I've got him contained. Are you coming out, sir?'

'I'm on my way. Keep him contained, start a dialogue. We'll sort it out.'

A dialogue: the traditional way of keeping a gunman's thoughts away from his gun, of persuading him to see reason. This one would be conducted through a loudhailer. Jean raised it to her lips.

'Rodney Maskell. This is Inspector Darblay. We're here,

quite a number of us, and we have this cottage surrounded. You're not going anywhere, so you'd better start to think about that. We have two armed policemen out here. Now you've discharged a firearm, but so far you haven't hurt anybody. Before somebody does get hurt – and it might be you – you'd better put that gun down and come out.'

His answering shout was hoarse and angry. 'You bloody woman cop! I'll come out when I want to. My daughter Maureen's with me. Your bloody gunmen won't risk shooting me and hitting her.'

Beck appeared, with a terrified Madge Maskell; Jean waved them back, out of sight. The police doctor got out of his car and approached, but before Jean could speak to him another shot had roared out over her head, followed by yet another as one of the Firearms Officers moved forward.

'You bloody woman cop!' Maskell shouted. 'You and your men better go away. I've had enough. I'm going to kill myself and my daughter now, unless you get your men away from here. You want to watch? Free show. I'll do it. The two of us have got nothing to live for. Nothing!'

Jean had moved to the doctor's side. She whispered to him, and got a pessimistic answer. She was more alarmed inside than she would let anyone see. The disembodied voice on her radio said that Superintendent Lake was on his way, but out of contact. Jean urged it to try to get a traffic patrol to intercept and hurry him. 'We need him here, very fast.'

In the top-floor room, Maureen was half-lying on the bare floor, choking on the aspirins he had given her. 'Da, I need water to swallow,' she moaned.

'We've no water. I'm sorry. Come on. We're going to escape, you and me. I'll work out a way.'

A quivering voice came over the loudhailer. 'Rodney. Maureen. It's me. This is your mother, Maureen. Listen, I know you love her, Rodney. I know I kept her from you. I won't do that no more. Just come out. Or let Maureen come out. I'll do anything you want.'

'You lying bitch!' came the answering shout. Both barrels went off, hitting the low wall behind which Jean and the others were crouching.

'Jesus!' cried Madge, and collapsed against Parrish, who at a sign from Jean led her away, leaving Beck and Jean together in their shelter. Beck looked at his watch.

'Mr Lake should be here by now. Shall I try and find out where he is?'

'The Super won't save you, Joseph.'

'It's his experience in situations like this that counts, boss,' the tactless Beck replied, and Jean, fraught as she was, came very near to losing her temper. Instead she said, 'Go away, Joseph.' It was no time for a private fracas. She saw the ambulance arriving. A journalist from the local paper crawled up to her, notebook at the ready, and was sent brusquely away. There was no sign of Lake; she would have to carry this operation through herself.

In the cottage, Maskell said to the wilting child, 'There's a way out of this – if you won't faint on me with your migraine. Will you?'

'I'm not going to faint,' she whispered.

He was talking hurriedly, urgently. 'They'll think I'm threatening your life. I'll put the gun to your head, pretend I'm going to shoot you if they don't let us go. That's it. You just walk very slowly in front of me, downstairs, and out back. I'll be behind you, with the gun. I'll tell them to get back. Then we walk slowly to t'car . . .'

'Dad, you won't shoot me?'

'No, Maureen.' His long, fond look told her he meant it, and made up her mind for her. She said, 'I won't do what you tell me, Da. And I'm going to leave this room now, Da.'

His face, absorbed in fantasy, changed suddenly. 'You can't.'

'How will you stop me, Da?'

'You will *not* leave, Maureen.' He turned the gun on her; she faced him without flinching.

'You said you won't shoot?'

'No. I won't. *They*'ll shoot you, *they*'ll kill you. They know you're part of me . . .' He turned away. 'I'm reaching a decision. Give me a moment, one moment.' He was looking out of the window, taking in the forces ranged against him. Maureen watched him, waiting for his decision.

'I don't think we'll escape, Maureen,' he said at last. 'I

reluctantly conclude that. But they won't have me to capture. Neither me, nor you, the innocent in all this. We're joined by love, Maureen. Will you remember that? Because it will always be so. Remember, please, for all time, that I love you, dearest child.'

There was something in his tone that made her believe him. They exchanged a long look before he said, 'It's time to go. You lead the way. Don't turn round.'

To Jean, crouching behind the wall, it seemed as though everything happened at once. The back door of the cottage opening, Maureen coming out nervously and slowly, advancing to the middle, turning with a scream as a shot fired inside the house sent birds flying upwards in a frightened cloud.

Maskell staggered out, walking like an automaton, blood pouring from a terrible wound in his chest. Suddenly he crumpled and fell, as Maureen screamed again.

'Oh God, no,' Jean said.

'How the hell did this happen?' Lake asked. 'Weren't you able to make any dialogue at all with him?' She was miserably aware of his angry face, of the fact that Beck and Parrish had turned away from her. No support from them. The other men were glancing at her, the doctor, the ambulance men. To Lake she said, 'We simply didn't have time to develop a dialogue.'

'Let's talk about you, not "we",' he said roughly. 'Didn't you attempt to negotiate any deal with him? What went wrong?'

'You can see what went wrong, sir.' The back-answer was a cover for her feeling of utter flatness and defeat. A few more brusque remarks, and Lake left her to give orders to Beck before going back to the station.

'City or County morgue, boss?' he asked.

'City. Organize Mrs Maskell to identify body, wait here for Chief Inspector Morell.'

'Yes, boss.'

'Sergeant Beck!' At her sharp recall he turned back, to see her get out of the Escort and face him.

'Sergeant Beck. Listen to me. Don't you ever call me "boss" again. Call me "ma'am". Don't ever open a car door for me, or an office door. I'll do that myself. Don't ever put your hand out to help me climb over anything. Is that clear?'

'Yes, ma'am.'

'I'm here to stay, Joseph. So forget all those jokes about women, and your snide looks. Then we'll be all right, you and me. Understood?'

'Yes, ma'am.'

He watched her drive off, his face thoughtful. She had just said what, without knowing it, he had been waiting for her to say, and it was the right thing. Now he knew where he stood.

From the station, later that evening, she telephoned Tom at home.

'I've cooked a bloody capon, so far without burning it,' he told her.

Her voice trembled on the edge of tears as she said, 'Thanks, love.'

'What sort of day have you had?'

'Not too good. I'm coming home now, love.'

'I'll put the kettle on,' he said cheerfully.

'Thanks, love,' she said again, and meant it.

chapter three

Sergeant Beck and Sergeant Melchett were sitting in their parked Ford Escort. They appeared calm observers of the street scene, but their eyes never moved from the small figure toddling along, her shopping trolley behind her, like a very elderly pony drawing a light carriage. Melchett informed his hand radio, 'She's arrived.'

'On time as usual,' Beck observed. They settled down to watch her turn into the entrance of a yard where ten used cars stood, each bearing a placard advertising itself as a bargain. A sign on the wall proclaimed *Jimmy Jason Automobiles*. The little old woman crossed the yard and entered a hut-like office on the far side of it.

'Right,' said Melchett. 'We hang around till she comes out.'

In the tiny cluttered office, Jimmy Jason himself was also watching old Doris's approach. A portly man, with an air of good living matching his expensive suit, he could have passed for a respectable town councillor rather than the villain he actually was. His assistant villain, Eddie Bass, equally big but rougher in appearance, rubbed oily hands on his overalls. He was Jimmy's chief mechanic and partner in deals connected sometimes with stolen cars, more often with stolen spare parts. Jason gestured with his thumb.

'It's her. Out.'

Bass said, 'You owe me the money. I want to see you earn it. Anyway, she'd see me go.'

'All right, then. But not a sound from you – and not a grin, either.' He opened the door to admit Doris, saying winningly, 'Hello, dear.'

The old woman beamed up at him. 'Hello, Jimmy.' Eighty-one years of hard living had not quenched the cheerfulness of her spirit. She greeted Eddie. 'How are you, dear?'

'Not too good.' Eddie knew that he must not give the impression that all was well with Jimmy Jason Automobiles. Jason was almost bowing Doris into the office, clearing and dusting a chair for her with the gallantry of a Walter Raleigh. 'Ta,' she said. 'I thought I'd pop by, seeing as you said it's important.'

'It is, Doris. Now – today, do I get to make you a cuppa?'

'No, dear, not today – this is me on me way to work.'

Jason avoided catching Bass's eye as he said heavily, 'Doris, you've got to know my many tales of woe over the years, haven't you?'

'Yes, dear.' Bass was already having to suppress a smirk.

'And you know that there's some of us singled out, for whatever reason, to experience this world only as a Vale of Tears.' He was proud of that touch.

'I know, Jimmy. I know Providence has given you the thin end, always.'

Jason sighed. 'Well, I'll tell you what happened. I bought a motor. Turned out it was stolen, would you believe. Cops turned up, took it away – double bastards. It was going to be a quick turnaround. I had a customer lined up for it. Fundamentally, Doris, I'd already spent the profits, written a few cheques. Well, you know I've been done before for bad cheques. Can you help me?' he ended with a convincing impersonation of boyish frankness.

'How much this time, Jim?'

He hesitated. 'I hardly dare tell you.'

'Say it, Jimmy, face it.'

Hanging his head, he muttered, 'I need eight hundred pounds.'

Far from seeming shocked, Doris asked briskly. 'Would a cheque in the post by Monday suffice?'

He put his hand over hers, his voice husky with simulated emotion. 'You're no less than my eternal treasure – I mean that.'

This time Bass's mirth almost overflowed, and he had to disguise it with an artificial attack of coughing. Doris gazed at him with concern.

'Are you all right, Mr Bass?' she inquired.

He assured her that it was only a frog in the throat, and managed to control himself until she had left before letting it out, not joined by Jason.

'Oh dear, oh dear! "I've experienced in this world only a vale of tears . . . You're no less than my eternal treasure . . .".' He wiped his running eyes. Jason eyed him coldly.

'Laugh, you stupid pig. Know something? If you live to be a hundred, you'll never be half the villain that old lady is.'

Doris, glowing with a sense of righteousness, was going off up the street. Behind her the Ford Escort began to move slowly.

They tracked her to the Hall Electric factory, four miles outside the town of Hartley, where she worked as a tea lady. In the Cashier's Department, Doris's arrival was awaited by three men: the Company Cashier, the Company Secretary, and young Detective Sergeant Davies of the Hartley CID, in plain clothes. As he waited, he thought of his dogs, two greyhounds and two whippets, the pride of his heart and his chief preoccupation. His mates were always teasing him about having no girl friend. But with what those dogs cost to keep, he couldn't afford a girl friend, and he didn't really care. The dogs were a lot more satisfactory to think about, when a chap had so much hanging about to do . . .

The cashier was looking at his watch. 'She's usually here ten forty-five on the dot. This office is her first call. Then the directors' suite, then out to the workers.'

Davies switched his mind from dogs, and produced from his pocket a written affidavit, clearing his throat.

'Then I'll read you this, gentlemen. *I, Detective Sergeant Davies of Hartley CID, produce for you, David Harcourt, Company Cashier, Hall Electric, of the Industrial Estate, Hartley, in the presence of this witness Donald Ferguson, Company Secretary, the eleven in number cheques which you, David Harcourt, have personally typed out for signature by one of your directors, a Mr Mason. You will now hand these cheques, as has been your custom for the last four years approximately, to Mrs Doris Latham to take to Mr Mason at the directors' suite across the yard.*'

Harcourt touched the cheques laid out on his desk. 'I confirm that there are eleven cheques here. Ah! She's here.' Doris entered, pushing a rattling tea trolley laden with crockery.

'Morning, Mr Ferguson, Mr Harcourt. D'you want your teas here, Mr Ferguson?'

Ferguson was ready with an answer. 'Yes, Doris – just this morning. And no sugar, I'm going to start saccharin again.'

Doris spooned sugar into the teas she had poured. 'One with two, one without. Would this gentleman like tea?'

Davies politely refused, and Harcourt handed her the bundle of cheques.

'Here you are, Doris, the cheques for Mr Mason.' She thanked him and backed herself out of the office, pulling the tea trolley after her. When the door had shut Harcourt said, 'Give her five minutes.'

'You understand, gentlemen,' Davies warned them, 'this may be the first of a number of Fridays when we'll have to go through this routine until she tries one on.'

'Oh, we do understand that, Sergeant,' Harcourt answered.

'How much d'you reckon she's stolen so far?' Davies asked him.

'Well, we're nearly back the full four years through the books. It's a fortune.' Davies whistled.

The five minutes were hardly up when the telephone rang. Harcourt answered it. 'Yes, Mr Mason.' His face lit up as he listened. Then, 'I'll repeat this in front of witness and Sergeant Davies. You are informing me that old Doris Latham placed twelve cheques before you for signature, not eleven. Eleven being the number given to her by myself on leaving this office. Thank you, sir.' Before he could hang up, Davies said urgently, 'Can he hold on to her?'

Harcourt said into the telephone, 'Can you hold on to her, sir? I believe the police sergeant wishes to come across now and make the arrest. Thank you, sir.'

Davies hurried out, after thanking them for their cooperation, and Harcourt turned to Ferguson.

'Eighty-one years of age! Staggering.'

Inspector Jean Darblay was not pleased to hear that old Doris was occupying one of Hartley's classic Victorian cells. She asked Beck, sharply, why the hell the old lady had been brought there.

'Begging your pardon, ma'am, why not?' Beck had never called her 'boss' since the Marly Cottage incident.

'Because Hall Electric's off our map.'

'Aye, but she lives in Hartley. Gaynor Road.'

'You could've taken her to City Road,' Jean snapped. 'Why was she brought here without so much as a word on the air to ask what I feel about it?'

Melchett said, 'I'm sorry, ma'am, I don't understand what the problem is.'

Jean turned on him. 'Sergeant Melchett, it's her age. This is an eighty-one-year-old woman, arrested for the first time in her life. She'll probably have a heart attack and expire here in my station. And then *I* get to deal with all the attendant press publicity – *Eighty-one-year-old dies in police custody – my* custody. Because you didn't think to take her into City Road when these thefts are a city case. Because you didn't think to call through and tell me you were bringing her here.'

The three of them, Beck, Melchett and Davies, were sheepishly silent.

'All right,' Jean told Beck and Davies, 'you two can go.' Followed by Melchett, she went to the iron door of the old cell, and looked in through the hatch. Old Doris was reclining, half-collapsed, on the bench, staring into space. Jean didn't like the look of her at all.

'Well, Sergeant Melchett, you've now involved me. Let's hear about it. How did it work?'

'Last four and a half years, she's been one of three tea ladies at Hall Electric. Over that time, every Friday morning after she's served tea to Company Cashier, she crosses yard to directors' suite in separate office block to serve them teas.'

'And – ?'

'Cashier says it was about four years ago he started asking her to take all his cheques for signature across with her to directors' suite.'

Jean reflected that such an arrangement would hardly have happened in her father's time as a factory executive. But firms didn't have office boys any more, only any messengers they could get, such as very old ladies.

'She stole some chequebooks,' Melchett went on. 'Once every month or so she'd type out an extra cheque for this boy friend of hers, slip it into the pile. The director, with a pile of cheques which he thinks have just come fully scrutinized by the Company Cashier, just signs it, and it's posted off with the other cheques.'

Jean raised her eyebrows. 'Did you say boy friend? Eighty-one and she's got a boy friend?'

'Worse than that, her boy friend we know – Jimmy Jason.'

'The bent car dealer? He got the cheques?'

'Aye, but we can't prove it. Not till she talks, that is. Chief Inspector Wigan is coming here – he can tell you the whole story.'

'How much has been nicked?'

'They've not completely traced back through the full four years in the books. The figure so far is thirty-one thousand pounds.'

'*What?*'

'That's right. And this is the last complication. Although we're sure the money ended up in Jimmy Jason's pocket, the cheques weren't made out to him.'

'Who, then?'

'Arthur Hill.'

'Any clue from the computer?'

'Nothing.'

'I see. All right, let's have a word with her.' Melchett unlocked the heavy door, and they went in. Doris straightened herself. There were signs of tears on her face, but she was doing her best to look cheerful and social. There was the faintest gleam of relief at seeing a woman coming to question her, and a reasonable-looking one at that, not something like you'd expect to see, from one of those films about concentration camps.

Jean advanced into the cell. 'I'm Inspector here at Hartley, Doris.'

'Aye, I heard all these men have got a woman in charge.'

'Have we got the name of your doctor, Doris? Has anyone asked you?'

'It's Doctor Bannerjee. Railton Parade. I haven't been to him for a year or more. Is he still about?'

'We know him. Well, what have you been up to, then? Stolen some money?'

Doris must have expected the question, but somehow, put like that, it didn't sound right. 'Stolen'? Oh, no. It was quite different. She was being asked nicely, so perhaps the lady Inspector would understand, even though it was hard to explain. 'I haven't taken any for myself, not one halfpenny,' she said. 'I've not benefited for me. So I hope it's not too serious.' She allowed herself a quavering smile.

'Are you going to tell me all about it in a statement?' Jean asked quietly.

'Well, whatever you like. I'll tell you all about it, except I'll not implicate my friend in his misfortune.'

'What misfortune?'

It was Melchett who answered. 'She has a story that the other suspect continually told her he'd go out of business unless he received the moneys.'

'Did he . . . has she named him?'

'No, she won't.'

Jean turned to Doris, who was looking from one to another of them, not quite catching all they said. 'We have the name of your friend, so it's not down to you to implicate him. But could you do us a favour, dear, tell us everything you're prepared to tell us, and we'll write it down?'

Doris's face clouded. 'Well, I'll have to have a think about that.'

'Aye, well, you do.' As Jean turned away Doris asked, 'Is there any chance of tea?'

'Yes, we can get you a cup, before your lunch.'

'Oh, I really would like one!'

'While it's brewing up, could you tell me some things I can write down about your goings-on, then?'

'I'll tell you anything you want to know, except the name of my friend.'

'All right.' Jean beckoned Melchett outside the cell and said, 'Give me ten minutes with her and then bring us a pot of tea.'

Melchett hesitated. 'Ma'am. May I respectfully remind you that this is a major case? The DCI initiated it. I think you should delay your taking a statement until the DCI gets over here from City.'

'I want the statement down now, in case this old girl drops dead, and, with respect, if the DCI was so shining keen about it, he should have issued instructions to you to take her to City. As it is, she's here, and it's Friday. She's certainly going to be with us over the weekend. I'm stuck with that, and her. I'm involved. And I'm going to have her statement. Get the tea.'

Melchett sighed, but not audibly, and went.

Doris brightened at the sight of the tea, but Jean's questions were not at all to her liking. A great block in her mind stopped her answering the most important of them.

'Now let's get this right,' Jean said. 'You met this gentleman, whom we shall call Mr X, four years back. He pitched you the first of many hard-luck stories. You decided you liked him. You wanted to help him. So you stole a company chequebook and started typing out cheques for him and then slipping them into the Friday pile for the director to sign. Is that it?'

Doris nodded. 'Yes.' She didn't mind admitting that much.

'It's critical to your defence, Doris, whether you dreamt up the scheme of stealing chequebooks and slipping cheques into the pile, or whether Mr X dreamt it up.'

'I admit I worked it out.' All right to say that, too, she thought. 'It's really the only bad thing I did on this.'

Jean couldn't keep the surprise out of her voice. 'What d'you mean, it's the only bad thing you did?'

'I told you, I didn't keep any of the money for myself – it were given away.'

Jean's patience with this difficult case was infinite. 'Doris,' she said gently, 'how much d'you think's involved? How much of Hall Electric's money did you pass on to Mr X?'

'I don't know.'

'Can't you give us a guess?'

'Oh, it must have been several hundred pounds.'

'Doris, the company accountants have gone back nearly the four years, and what d'you think it comes to? Thirty-one thousand-odd pounds.'

She had managed to amaze Doris, and it was genuine amazement. 'Never! That's not true.'

'It is true. You're in serious trouble, dear.'

Doris stirred the dregs of cooling tea round in her cup, her face a blank. Then she said, 'But I never took a penny for myself, except the odd five pounds I give to the orphanage.'

'What orphanage?'

'Well, sometimes when I'd see Mr X he'd say "Ta" for saving his life as it were, and give me a five pound, or a ten pound, for the orphanage – the council, St Kilda's.'

'You mean the children-in-care home?'

'It used to be orphanage. I takc thc five pounds Mr X give me and knock on door and say, "Here's a five-pound note for comfort for the kiddies . . ."' Suddenly she was in tears, sobbing out, 'I never took a penny for myself. I give it all away . . . to him . . . to the orphans.'

Jean touched her shoulder lightly. She was beginning to wish even more heartily that the poor old thing had been taken to City; and yet she knew that she of all people could make something of Doris's extraordinary attitude to her crime. If anyone could. 'There's no point in just upsetting yourself, dear,' she said. 'Come on, try and stop crying.'

After a few moments of sniffing, Doris bravely dried up.

'I was an orphan,' she said, 'brought up by me Salvation Army aunt, all cornets and hymns and hellfire. And all that bloody cleanliness! she even washed the cat once a week. I think I did this to curse her memory, you know. It's the sort of thing that if she'd been alive and heard it, it'd have killed her. Good!' Her own vehemence broke her down again. Jean waited for her crying to quieten, then said, as gently but firmly as a nurse, 'I want to start right from the beginning. Let's make it your statement. Now, you tell me if you're prepared to say this. *I, Doris Anne Latham, of sixty-one Gaynor Road, Hartley . . .*'

Chief Inspector Wigan's official relationship with Jean was an odd one. Their status was equal, yet unequal, he outranking her as belonging to City but also being in charge of her CID. The station itself was her domain; in it, she could, and did, tell him what he could and could not do in it. He, a man who enjoyed authority and respect, was not happy with the situation. She was his junior, and a woman, two things he found hard to take. He let her see his resentment clearly, and she reacted in the only sensible way, by staying polite but firm and refusing to be put down. That way, he would at least come to respect her; in time, and if his prejudices were not too inflexible to be modified.

He thought she had moved too fast on the questioning of Doris, and told her so. It would have been better, wiser, to wait until he arrived before taking Doris's statement. As it was, she'd put the idea of sheltering Jimmy Jason behind the fictitious personality of Mr X into Doris's head. 'I think *I*'d have pressed her quite forcibly on her accomplice being Jimmy Jason,' he said. 'As it is, she's calmly drinking tea and saying she's told *you* everything she's going to say.'

'I think she has.'

'Well, I'm asking you, where do we go from here?'

'Since the decision was made to place her here without reference to me, in my custody, then clearly I'm involved. And I'll continue to be involved.'

Wigan met her straight gaze. After a moment he shrugged.

'Well then, it looks like me aiding you.' His tone implied that it ought to have been very much the other way round.

A sad-looking man, like a shabby dachshund, had been brought in by Wigan, and was conducted to Jean's office to tell them about the cheques he had cashed for Jason. His name was George Moult, pub landlord, accustomed to cashing something like a dozen cheques a week for customers. No, he'd never asked the man for any proof of identification; if he said he was Arthur Hill, then he must be, because the cheques never bounced. Yes, he had asked why the man didn't use a bank, and was told he'd once been very badly let down by one. And anyway, Hill was a good bloke who always bought a couple of bottle of whisky when he cashed a cheque. Yes, he was prepared to help the police make out a Photofit picture – spare-part surgery with snapshots, guaranteed to make everybody look like Frankenstein's monster – that was what he thought of it, but he'd help.

As his drooping back view receded, Wigan said, 'I've got a feeling we should go and pick up Jason.'

'But you said you had absolutely nothing on him.'

Wigan set his lips in a stubborn line. 'I want to talk to him.'

Jean's conviction that talking to Jason would not be a good idea was confirmed by Jason's attitude when they interviewed him at his office.

'Full name, please.' Wigan wore his most official face. Jean was glancing round the office, noting the general clutter, last month's calendar sheet not torn off, brimming ashtrays, half-open drawers with documents spilling out of them. She always itched to attack such places, but mess and untidiness were no evidence of criminality. There was plenty of that in the general air of the man, self-satisfied and covertly insolent. To Wigan's question he replied, 'It's in two-foot lettering in front of t'shop – *Jimmy Jason.* Would you like me to spell it?'

Wigan ignored the crack. 'Home address?'

'Sixteen Stapely House, Ulster Road.'

'You had a visit this morning from an old lady, Mrs Doris Latham.'

'Did I?'

'Did you?'

'Yes.'

Jean asked, 'Can you tell us why she came here?'

Jason rocked back in his chair and lit a cigarette. 'She collects for a charity,' he said casually. 'What she calls her orphanage. St Kilda's, the council care home. She drops by once a week, and I give her a few bob.'

Wigan said, enjoying it, 'You won't be seeing her for a while, Mr Jason. We've arrested her for a series of cheque robberies involving in excess of thirty thousand pounds.'

Jason's thick eyebrows went up, but he showed no sign of shock. 'You're kidding?'

'No.' Wigan was watching him closely, and getting nothing from it.

'Okay. So what d'you want from me?'

'You've been in trouble before.'

Jason smiled patiently. 'Oh come on, Inspector. These are

the days of microchips and teletext, and home computers, and busmen getting up at six to study sociology on Open University. You can't come flat-footed in here and say, "You've been in trouble before – I'll write your confession. You sign it with your usual X." '

Jean could see that Wigan was getting angry. 'We know Latham saw a lot of you,' he snapped. 'We know the physical description of the person who cashed the cheques at a pub doesn't fit your description, but we also know he's an associate of yours.'

'Well, I say you know nothing, the two of you.' His glance flickered across Jean contemptuously. 'Otherwise you'd be putting the manacles on. You're trying one on, and it's not working. So what's next?'

Jean turned her back on him and went swiftly out, followed by Wigan. She couldn't resist saying what had been in her mind before they went in. 'Not a good move.'

'It was,' Wigan returned sharply. 'He's made me angry. I'm going to get him.'

Further patient questioning of Doris produced no more results. There was no way one could browbeat anyone as old and as pathetic. One tactful question after another produced nothing but loyal defence of Mr X. 'He's a poor unfortunate man who's been struck every blow in the armoury of fate. There just *are* some people like that, that are blocked on every move they try to do, no matter how hard they try. I don't think he's had one happy day in his life.'

'I should think he had a hilarious one the day he met you,' Jean remarked, but sarcasm was wasted on Doris.

'His business was always in trouble. No one cared if he lived or died.'

A picture of the smug, obviously bent man in the cluttered office flashed through Jean's mind. She sat down and tried another line with the stubborn old woman.

'Now look, Doris, he's a big man, it's not as if he was a helpless invalid. And by the law of averages, if you're in the car business, despite recession, petrol prices, all that, you've got to fall on your feet sometimes and make a few bob.'

'Well, he didn't.' Jean pounced.

'So you're admitting it's Jimmy Jason – not denying it when I said he's a big man in the car business?' All she got for her neat trick was a disappointed look.

'You tried to trap me,' Doris accused. 'Well, that's mean of you and I'm still saying nothing.'

Jean's patience was wearing thin, though she mustn't show it. It had been a long, trying day. Wigan's presence was always a strain. And this intractable old person was beginning to make her doubt her own powers of persuasion. It was a relief to snap, 'Jimmy Jason is a rotten little villain who saw a good thing, and he trapped you!'

Doris's face was a shut door. 'I'm saying nowt.'

'Well, keep thinking about it, because we're hoping you're going to change your mind.'

In the pause that followed the shut face became troubled, and the weary old eyes went to the wall clock. Perhaps she was weakening, becoming tired. But what she said at last was, 'Listen, missus, something very important, which I hardly dare mention, but it's worrying me sick. I told your sergeant I lived alone; well, I don't. It's my cat, Blackie. It's gone four o'clock, I'm worried. I'm usually home now, to give him his tin. What with me in here, what am I going to do about it? He may be ill if I don't turn up.'

Jean suppressed a sigh. 'Have we got your house key?'

'Yes.'

'I'll send the sergeant in with a note for you to sign, that you've instructed us to enter your house and feed your cat. Some time in the next couple of hours. Will that be all right?'

'Thanks very much. He'll find the tins on the dresser.'

Jean got up, and tried a last throw. 'Are you going to think about telling us about Jimmy Jason?'

'No, dear.' But Doris accompanied the rejection with a smile, because after all the police lady was being kind about poor Blackie.

chapter four

In the end it was Jean herself who undertook the feeding of Blackie, on her way home from the station that evening. She had picked up Tom in town, where he had been waiting for her after spending the afternoon at the firm he was to join as supervisor of coil windings. It was not a great job, much lower-paid than his previous one, but it was better than unemployment.

Together they stood at the door of Doris's so-called flat. It was a sight to make a housewife blanch, and Jean, under her uniform, was still a housewife. The furniture was junk, chairs with sagging seats, stained cushions, a rusty old gas stove, a chipped stone sink full of dirty dishes and unwashed milk bottles. The gas fire was badly broken, its filaments hanging crooked like old teeth; Jean noted it mentally as a potential danger to life. The square of threadbare carpet was ingrained with cat litter, spread from Blackie's tray, which had only too obviously not been cleaned out lately. Blackie himself, who had been sleeping on the dirty coverlet of the bed in the adjoining cupboard-like room, leapt down at their entry and ran to them with a welcoming cry.

Tom stooped to stroke him, then surveyed the room again.

'Good grief,' he said. 'She didn't spend much of her thirty thousand pounds here, did she?'

'She didn't spend any of it – gave every penny away.'

Tom whistled. 'And this is the so-called welfare state.'

'I see it all the time. This is par for the course for an old one living on her own. This place, reproduced hundreds of thousands of times around this country. You've always been protected, Tom – cottonwoolled like a Tory politician.'

Tom smiled. He had heard that before, in one form or another. 'If you say so.'

'I do. You feed the cat. It gets one whole tin, she says. The tins are on the dresser and the can-opener's in the table drawer. I'll wash this lot up.'

'You'll get yourself filthy.'

'Can't help it. I couldn't leave the place like this.' She looked at an apron draped over a chair, took in its grimed condition and decided against it, tackling the washing of the dishes and bottles with her uniform skirt and jacket well out of reach of splashes. The water was cold, the washing-up powder clogged, but anything was better than what she had found.

Tom looked up from the happily feeding cat. 'Jean – this job. AGC.'

'Yes?'

'It's not what I want.'

'*Now* he tells me,' she informed the cat.

'You were right, you know – I did panic and take it because it's gone six months since the redundancy.' Jean knew that something else was coming. Tom liked to lead up to things.

'When I was down the job centre I saw two jobs in the Social Services advertised. One was a council officer with duties of liaising with organizations like Help the Aged.'

'And the pay?'

'Look, at Speke Triumph I was a fully qualified design engineer. Barring miracles, I think it's going to be a long time before I get the same kind of job again. I've been thinking, instead of taking some job like this one at AGC, I should spend the waiting months doing something useful.' He was watching her anxiously for understanding and agreement.

'Like what?' she asked, noncommitally.

'Like helping old people who live in this kind of filth. Designing bits of cars and supervising coil winders doesn't do a lot for humanity.'

'It got us married. It bought our first house. It's helping to buy the new one.'

'I know that.'

'Well, that happens to mean a lot to me.' Her back was turned to him, her face invisible. He moved nearer to her.

'Jean, I don't want to be a supervisor of coil windings at AGC, for half the wage I got at Speke. I want to spend the next few months – well, maybe many months – doing a useful job. I'm glad I came to this place with you. It's helped me to find out what I really want. It . . . it doesn't have to be the Help the Aged job, there were others . . .'

She knew that he was waiting anxiously for her to answer, that it meant a lot to him what she said. It was not Jean's way to delay decisions, and Tom's happiness meant hers as well.

'Well,' she said briskly, 'all you have to do is phone AGC, tell them to stuff it, and say you're going to work for old ladies at half the price.'

'You're serious?' He could hardly believe it.

'I am.'

'Are you sure? I mean, to drop this just when we're buying a new house . . . You're a hundred-per-cent positive?'

Her smile was bright and confident. 'Yes.'

Tom was no more given than she was to extravagant expressions of emotion. He bent to stroke Blackie, who was rubbing round his legs with loud purrs. 'This cat likes me,' he said. 'How long d'you think the old lady's going to jail for?' He eyed the cat speculatively.

Jean laughed. Tom was very vulnerable where animals and helpless things in general were concerned. 'Don't let's get stuck in our new straitened circumstances with another mouth to feed,' she said.

'How long will I go to jail for?' Doris was asking.

'I couldn't tell you,' Jean said. 'I don't know. Doris – tell me one thing. How did you meet this friend of yours in the first place?'

'I was in two hours' work, morning and afternoon, tea lady at Hall Electric. I needed some money. I advertised in local paper to take in sewing and alterations. Well, this man phones me. He's got three suits to alter, let out, 'cause he's put on weight. He was so kind, recommended me to his friends. It was through them I learned how he was always in financial trouble. That's the only crime I've done, I've helped a good man.'

'We know who it is, and he's a criminal.' Jean opened a folder. 'Have you ever seen one of these before, dear?'

Doris glanced at it idly. 'No.'

'It's called a Photofit. It was made up to the directions of the publican who cashed your cheques. It's a sort of rough likeness of the man Arthur Hill, that you wrote the cheques out to. Does this look like anyone you've met recently?'

'No.' Doris sounded sharp, for her. 'And it doesn't look like that name you mention, Jimmy Jason, so there.'

In the Intensive Care unit of Oakwood Hospital a man lay motionless, heavily bandaged, who very closely resembled the Photofit. Arthur Hill had been found in a quarry, in a pool of his own blood, the hammer with which he had been savagely attacked beside him. It was a panel-beater's hammer, and it had come from a garage. Jean looked at it, and at the almost lifeless man, and said to Chief Inspector Wigan, 'We pick up Jimmy Jason.'

Jason's office was as untidy as when Jean had last seen it, and now there was no Jason in it. The safe was gaping open.

'So,' Jean said, 'he's run so fast and scared he doesn't lock up.'

Wigan was investigating the safe's contents. He laid them out on the desk. A teapot, sugar-bowl and cream jug, antique silver, a bunch of teaspoons, a silver presentation trophy, two christening mugs and a large engraved salver. Why, Wigan wondered aloud, did thieves always invest their money in silver?

'Maybe they know a thing or two we don't.' Jean was looking through the documents on the desk. 'He's got out fast – obviously terrified for Hill's life. He'll have gone to London, I'd guess. Seven registration documents here, six cars in the yard – if it follows he's taken the seventh one, then we've got the registration number.' She picked up the telephone and alerted traffic patrol.

Old Doris looked very chirpy when Jean visited her cell next morning. She had had a better breakfast than she was used to, and a fair night's sleep. Jean had a feeling that the old woman's morale would be high, and she was right. She decided to go straight into the attack.

'Last night there was a serious development in your case. The man whose name was on the cheques you wrote has been badly beaten up. He's in intensive care at Oakwood Hospital. It's your friend, Jimmy Jason, that's responsible.'

Doris stared up at her unwaveringly. 'You keep walking in this door as if with a bowl of water, and asking me to be Pontius Pilate and wash my hands of him. Look, missus, you must stop lying to me.'

'What am I lying to you about?' Jean knew that she was going to need all her patience.

'You say a certain man has been attacked by my friend and he's in hospital. He'd no more do that kind of thing than attack me.'

It would have been almost funny, Jean thought, if it hadn't been so maddening. 'Look,' she said, 'this nonsense has really got to stop. You're involved with a villain with a record as long as the Bible you've been quoting. Why are you protecting him?'

'I mean,' Doris explained, her head on one side, bird-like, 'it's a question of what price you put on the important things in life. For five years I was alone in that room, before I got this job as tea lady at Hall Electric, and even then it was still that empty room every hour I wasn't at work. Then this man came into my life. Me, eighty-odd; he can't be more than fifty. And he used to sit in his place of work every day, and I could pop in any time, make him a cup of tea, and have a lovely chat. Always talked about the good and bad old days. His dad and his grandad worked in Pharoah's Mill up t'hill, and he could remember his dad crying the day it closed. A grown man crying, fancy.'

'What are you saying, Doris?'

'Now you call this friend of mine a criminal. You want me to stand in a court and betray him. I can't. I don't care what you say he's done. He's been my one and only friend, and I love him.'

They exchanged a long look, Doris triumphant in her own impeccable reasoning, secure in her sense of right, utterly blind to the facts and to the reality of her own situation. Perhaps only a *fait accompli* would convince her. Jean shrugged. 'All right.'

The collapse of the emotional argument she had been building so happily threw Doris. She had been prepared for more attacks on her idol, not for this apparent surrender. Was it over – had she won? Would this alarming lady say she had been very brave, and nothing would be done to her friend, and she could go home now? After all, she'd been very kind and understanding about Blackie.

'He's used to eating first thing in the morning,' she said.

Jean, her thoughts on the capture of Jason, came to with a start. 'What?'

'Blackie. He gets half a tin in the morning, one at night. Who's going to feed him?'

'I'll drop by, or I'll get one of my men to. Okay?'

She went herself, of course, drawn by her sense of responsibility to the helpless old woman – not that she had asked for it. The room, abandoned now for twenty-four hours, looked even worse than the first time she had seen it, and foodstuffs somewhere were obviously beginning to go off. Blackie was there, purring, looking affectionately up at her as she washed his saucer and put it down with fresh food in it. But he merely glanced at it and leaped up on to a chair, where he arranged himself for sleep. Jean drew her own conclusions.

'Somebody's already fed you, darling.'

The door of the tiny bedroom was not in the same position as it had been when she and Tom had been there before. Very softly she backed out of the living-room. In her car, she spoke to the station. 'Number sixteen, Gaynor Road. Instruct Davies and Melchett to get here fast – very fast.'

Behind the ragged curtain of the sitting-room window, Jason was watching her, an iron fire-poker in his hand.

He was still there when Melchett and Davies arrived. Jean had told them they could have the arrest, and they were delighted. Melchett vanished round the side of the house to look after the back door while Davies approached the front door. Suddenly it shot open, and the big form of Jason hurtled out, striking Davies with the heavy poker as he passed him. The boy fell, clutching his arm, and struggled up in time to see Jason run to a car parked several yards up the street, scramble into it, and start it up. But Melchett, who had heard the noise and turned back, was after him, clutching the car door-handle, only to be flung off as it started . . .

Jean walked into the station to be greeted by Sergeant Parrish from his desk. 'There's a chase on. Melchett and Davies on the dual carriageway after Jason.'

'Got past them, did he?'

. . . They followed the chase by way of Melchett's personal radio. Jason had left the stolen car, was on foot. He had blocked the way of a traffic warden mounted on a Honda, assaulted the warden and stolen the machine.

'We've lost him. We've lost our mobile,' reported Melchett. 'Any mobiles area Junction Road, Green's Lane? Over.'

'What d'you mean, you've lost your car? What the hell's going on?'

'Can't discuss now. In pursuit of suspect. Over and out.'

It was several long minutes before another report came, this time from Davies.

'We have him. We have Jason.'

The tense chase had ended, dramatically, in the canal. Jason could hardly have hoped to make a getaway on a borrowed Honda he could scarcely ride, but he was too desperate, and basically too stupid, to recognize it. In his final struggle on the narrow plank walkway across the canal lock, he, Melchett and the moped crashed into the canal. Now there was no more running, nothing else he could do. Meekly he followed the dripping Melchett to the towpath.

Escorted by Sergeant Beck, and followed by Melchett, Davies, and Jean, Jason arrived at his cell door and was ushered in. Eyes had watched him from the door-hatch of another cell: Doris's eyes. Jean knew, and went to her once Jason was locked in. She was sitting quietly, looking at nothing in particular. As Jean entered she turned her head.

'I see you've captured him,' she said.

'Yes. Well, now we've got him, will you make a statement?'

Doris set her mouth stubbornly.

'I might as well tell you, love, we don't actually *need* a statement from you,' Jean told her. 'He's talked like a blithering parrot, on and on. Told us the assault on Arthur Hill was performed by one Edward Bass. Hill's recovering, you might be pleased to hear. Sure you wouldn't like to get in your side of the story?'

'No, dear.'

'Loyal to the end, eh?'

Doris answered with serene dignity. 'It's not loyalty, dear, it's principles.'

Jean had seldom felt so baffled. 'Well,' she said, 'I'll see about your elevenses.' As she moved towards the door, Doris said, 'The sergeant says I'm going to court tomorrow morning. What'll happen there?'

'There'll be charges laid, and then you'll be remanded to one of the nearest prisons.'

Doris's look was wistful. 'Can't I come back here after court to wait my trial? I mean, apart from having to sit here with me burden of guilt, I've really quite liked the company.'

Jean could hardly believe her ears. 'You want to be remanded to our custody – to come back here?'

'Oh yes, dear. Definitely.'

Can it be true, Jean thought, we're a home from home? Aloud she said, 'I'll see what I can do.' At the door she turned and said something she had never said before in those circumstances. 'We've quite enjoyed having you here, Doris.'

The old woman smiled. 'Thank you, dear.'

'It was true,' Jean said to Tom that night. 'All right, she was as stubborn as a mule and you couldn't make her see reason, even when it was staring her in the face. But she meant well and she was honest, in a wild sort of way. Bit of a change from most of them.'

Tom smiled. 'Feminine logic?' He could often get a rise out of Jean that way.

She shrugged. 'If you like. Mother defends child whatever it's done. Pity she had to waste her protection on a right villain like Jason.'

Tom usually enjoyed his coffee, but he was letting it grow cold.

'What will she get?' he asked.

'How do I know? Depends. Hardly a suspended sentence, with a sum like that involved. More likely to be an open prison

– though what's the use of sending an eighty-one-year-old to any sort of prison? Oh, well. I'll keep an eye on her.'

Tom knew his wife. What she did for old Doris would be done not out of sentimentality but out of real concern. Perhaps it was impossible for a woman not to become involved to some extent, even when she was as tough and efficient as Jean.

Comfortable before his own fire, he watched his wife, sitting relaxed in a flowing caftan of deep pink which suited her. Her newly washed hair stood out fluffily round her face, and the tired lines round her eyes were smoothed out. She looked ten years younger than she did in uniform, he thought.

But her mind was still on old Doris. 'It's a poor sort of reflection on a person's life when she enjoys a few days in the nick.'

'Aye.' He was seeing again the squalid room and smelling its rank odour. 'But I'm not surprised, living in a filthy hole like that.'

'Oh, you'll see plenty the same, don't worry, if you sign on with the Social Services. And worse. That was a palace compared with some. Drink your coffee – unless something's the matter with it?'

'No, it's fine.' He drained the cold dregs, not tasting them, then came out with something he had been trying to say.

'What'll happen to Blackie?'

'Who?'

'The cat. Doris's cat.'

'Oh, him. We'll get the RSPCA to put him down. She'll never go back to that place, and nobody else there'd take him.'

Tom was not looking at her. 'We could.'

Jean stared, and laughed. 'Tom Darblay! Are you on about that again? I told you—'

'We can do without another mouth to feed, I know. Well, that doesn't make sense, does it, if the poor thing only gets through a couple of tins of stuff a day.'

'We *are* moving house, you know.'

'He'd take that in his stride, wouldn't he? With decent food and a bit of comfort, he'd go anywhere, I reckon.'

'Told you so, did he?'

'Well . . . he was very affectionate. When they're like that with strangers they're easy to settle in. And she can't have had him all that long – he's quite a young cat. Too young to be put down.'

'And who'd look after him, then?'

Tom was pleading. 'I'm not starting at AGC on Monday now. I'll be around quite a bit before I get anything else. He could stay in at first – you saw he was house-trained – and go out in the garden when he gets more used to the place. Jean?'

She laughed, but kindly. 'All right, you big soft thing. You can borrow a basket and fetch him tomorrow. I won't be responsible, mind; he'll be in your custody.'

He leaned forward and covered her hand with his. 'Thank you, love. I'd been worried.'

'You've got a social conscience, that's your trouble. You'd have been wasted on coil windings.' A pleasant thought came to her. 'I'll tell Doris tomorrow. That'll make her feel better about things.' She got up. 'Come on, it's late.' She held out her hands to him, and he took them, thinking how slender and girlish and pretty she looked, and how much kinder than her colleagues were allowed to suspect.

But he knew better than to tell her so.

chapter five

Visitors from London tended to be unwelcome at Hartley nick, and Detective-Sergeant Cole of the Flying Squad was no exception. Jean had already had a brush with Detective Superintendent Brunskill about her reluctance to lend him the men and facilities he wanted for his investigation of the body of a man shot through the head. She put down the telephone which had announced Cole's arrival, and looked at Brunskill.

'And what do I do with this Sergeant from London, sir? Accommodation, catering, what?'

'He's come up to identify the body. Do me a favour, keep him out from under our feet.'

Young Bentley, still red-faced from having been severely put down by Cole's sharp tongue on the drive from the London train, showed the visitor in. Introductions were performed, and Brunskill asked, 'You identified the body found by the cement drainage canal?'

Cole, a largish man with a pale expressionless face, replied, 'In the mortuary. I would have very much liked to have seen the body *in situ*.'

'We had everything we wanted from the site,' Brunskill said defensively. Jean saw that Cole was offended, and asked him, 'You've seen the murder scene?' He nodded, and she went on, 'Our belief is that he was shot locally, then moved there. If he'd been shot where he was found we'd have expected more blood near the body.'

'Yes, ma'am.'

Brunskill said, 'Now what can we do for you, Sergeant? You've identified the body, you can assist us – is this right? – with information about the deceased.'

Cole was looking at a point somewhere above Brunskill's

head. 'I have the relevant permission to remain here for as long as I can make a useful contribution.'

'We'll see how we can fit you in,' Brunskill said without warmth. 'I've got called to parade now, about a dozen who've just joined us. Perhaps you'd like to address them on the subject of the deceased?'

Cole said that he would like to.

Jean, surrounded by a dozen or so men of the Murder Squad and her two Sergeants, listened to Cole talking, and realized that despite local prejudice he was the right man for the case. The deceased had been identified as Arthur Roberts, address London, who had been staying at the Bell Inn, Ainslie Road, before the murder. Investigations had produced a police contact name – Sergeant Cole. The connection between the two was clearly and concisely explained.

'Arthur Roberts was a snout of mine for many years,' Cole told them. 'He was a highly intelligent man. At sixty, when most villains are getting punch-drunk with stir, he was at the height of his powers. He was a snout to me – that is, he gave information to me – about firms he didn't like. His real occupation was as a bag draughtsman. We know he planned six major bank robberies in London in the last five years – he may have planned as many as sixteen. He was good enough to work that percentage and get away with it. If he came here, he had a good reason to do so. We have to find that reason, because that's what will lead us to his killer.'

Brunskill briefly summarized what they knew of Roberts's movements in the two days between his arrival from London and the finding of his body. Bed at the Bell Inn not slept in for two nights, nobody seemed to have spoken to him, no car hired. So Roberts must have walked to where he was found – if he was not picked up. It was up to the Murder Squad to get on to his tracks.

Jean volunteered to drive Cole round the area, to show him the lie of the land. He expressed his gratitude, and she knew that it was hard for him. She tried to help. 'We're both suffering from a little social leprosy at the moment,' she told him.

'How's that, ma'am?'

'Well – you know you're not really wanted. We get a murder in a blue moon. We don't want some smart outsider barging in, subtracting kudos, maybe solving it.'

'I want it solved,' Cole said grimly. 'But how do you come to be a social leper?'

'Just a small matter between me and Detective Superintendent Brumskill. Can I do anything for you?'

'Yes. I'd like to keep the Boy Scout who met me at the station.'

Jean smiled inwardly at this description of the 'boy' – eager, enthusiastic young Constable Bentley. She could imagine the bright conversation he would have tried to make while driving Cole, and the London man's dour replies. Bad luck on Bentley, but if Cole wanted him Cole should have him.

It was in fact worse luck for Bentley than she had envisaged, for Cole insisted that they do their reconnoitring of the district on foot, to gauge where Roberts might have gone on the two nights he had not slept at the Bell. Panting with exertion, he toiled over rough moorland behind the unrelenting Cole, answering questions, identifying farms, wishing earnestly that Cole had never set foot in Hartley, hoping he would soon go away again. The man hadn't a sympathetic bone in his body. Bentley was used to being put down, but not like this . . .

When they got back to the station there was news for Cole. A colleague in London had traced an association between Roberts and one Tony Cantwell, specialist in the conversion of stolen money into foreign currency. Jean saw a fleeting ray of satisfaction lighten Cole's face. Good. So he was human.

A moment later she was doubting it again. To her question about lunch, he answered, 'Is there a facility to prepare a vegetarian meal for myself – just a place to cut up a few vegetables?'

There was – the locker room, not that it had been used for that particular purpose before. There he produced from his briefcase a paper bag, and from the bag a collection of peeled vegetables which he began to cut up meticulously. Tea and coffee he refused. Jean shrugged. To her surprise, he asked, 'You don't mind me making this meal?'

'Of course not.'

'I only eat once a day, lunchtime.'

Poor devil, what a life, but if it suited him . . . Impelled by curiosity, she asked, 'How did you start the friendship with Roberts?'

Cole placed the chopped vegetables on a plate and poured some dressing from a small bottle on to the uninviting array. Jean guessed that he had made it up himself to his own prescription.

'It started ten years back,' he said. 'He became my regular snout for a couple of pounds slipped under a pub table. As I said, he only informed on people he didn't like. There were certain things I approved of in him. He'd had a lot of suffering in his life – he'd found strengths, rather than weaknesses, from it. His son was killed in a motorbike crash – I know that. He was a careful man; I liked that.'

He produced a twist of paper containing rock salt and added it to the dressing. Jean, fascinated, said nothing.

'He knew one day I'd arrest him. That was the only game he played – pretending I wouldn't. The rest was honest. We used to meet a couple of times a week in a pub – Fulham Road. He'd tell me about the books he was reading. Biographies – the lightweight sort. He had a nice house in Peckham. Had a little dog – looked like him, neat. It's not right that such a precise man should meet such an untidy death.' Suddenly polite, he offered the plate to Jean. 'Would you care for some?'

'Thank you, no,' she said gravely. 'I'll leave you to it.'

'You should try vegetarianism. Good for you, ma'am.'

'With the price of vegetables what it is? I couldn't afford it. But you might talk to our George Parrish – he lives on bacon rolls.'

Now almost confidential in his manner, Cole asked, 'D'you think we should tell the Senior Investigating Officer about the phone call? Roberts's movements?'

'No rush. How long can you stay here?'

'Three or four days. Longer if I produce something to the satisfaction of my bosses.'

'Mm. Not long.'

'I'll do it . . . find the reason Roberts came here. It's a small town.'

'It's a complicated one,' she pointed out. 'A close community. Families that have known each other for generations. They're cool with strangers.'

'So am I,' replied Cole with truth.

Cole's further investigation of the moors within a three-mile radius of the Bell was undertaken by car, to the relief of Bentley, even though he would have to drive to all the twenty farms contained in it. Jean had joined the expedition, as much to watch Cole in action as from her desire to be in at any discoveries that might be made. Their first visit was to Black Elm Farm, where Bentley pointed out the farm's owner, Arthur Dillon, unloading fertilizer from a truck. A cheerful man, obviously with nothing to hide, he greeted them and declared himself willing to help in any way he could. Cole produced Roberts's photograph.

'This man. Did you see him?'

'No. Local?'

'No. Last Monday, did you see or hear anything out of the ordinary? Trucks or cars passing that you happened to notice weren't local? Around midnight.'

Dillon laughed. 'I'd be in bed. Nine o'clock every night, head on the pillow. Up four-thirty every morning. Hey – wait a mo. Monday night, there was something. I'm one of those unfortunates that if they do get woke up they've got a dickens of a job getting back to kip again. Happened Monday night.'

'What happened?' Cole asked.

'A boat on the river woke me up. The river's down there, through the trees. Boats go on it. Must have been about midnight. Thought it'd come from Pollitts Farm – they got a couple of caravans they let out in summer, with a little outboard boat. It sounded something like that.'

'This isn't summer,' Jean pointed out.

'But,' Dillon said, 'if boat were going up river, it must stop at Pollitts, 'cause river isn't deep beyond there.'

'Have you ever heard a boat on the river before at midnight?' Cole asked.

'Don't recollect. It would have to have some kind of light on it, but I was in bed, so I didn't see.'

They thanked him and drove off. 'Who owns Pollitts Farm?' Cole inquired of Bentley.

'Pollitts Farm? Mr Garland. He's one of those property speculators. But he's never here now – lives in Norwich.'

Pollitts Farm had a *For Sale* notice on its wall, cancelled out by another saying *Sold Prior to Auction.* Knocking and ringing produced no reply, but Jean noticed two bottles of milk on the doorstep. She picked one up, and sniffed it. 'Fresh. Let's have a look through the windows.'

Round the side of the house they came to what was obviously the window of the living-room. It was bare of furniture, but on the floor were sleeping-bags, a primus stove, a teapot and mugs.

'Hippies or squatters?' ventured Bentley.

'Hippies or squatters wouldn't con a milkman into delivering milk,' Jean said. To Cole. 'What do you think, Gordon?' She was trying to humanize him by using his first name, as she did unofficially with her staff.

'Someone's coming back. We need a watch mounted.'

'Right. Roland, stay here. I'll get some others out to you.'

Bentley's plaintive gaze followed them as they went off in search of the river bank. There, tethered, was a small boat, with the name *Wayfarer II* painted on its stern. It was empty, yielding no clues. They went back to the Escort and returned to the station.

Inquiries by telephone produced interesting information from Cole's colleague in London. Mr Garland of Pollitts Farm was also known as Harold Durrant and George Pettit, with a police record attached to both names. He ran a restaurant in Soho and a large house in Norwich, and in 1973 had bought Pollitts Farm for a hundred and thirty thousand pounds. The date and the sum tied in instantly to Cole. 'The Taylor Security job, October '73. Two hundred thousand pounds. That adds up to a hundred and thirty thousand for the farm, seventy thou for Tony Cantwell to change the hot securities. Let's say Roberts, Cantwell and Garland bought the farm with the proceeds of the robbery, intending to sit on the asset for a few years, then put it up for sale. When the farm was sold it came to the split, and something happened. Maybe Roberts argued about his share, and got killed for it. That could be it.'

'We'll pass this to the Senior Investigating Officer,' Jean said.

'Yes, we'll have to.'

In the pub opposite the station the theory was discussed that evening between Jean, Cole and Brunskill, who was excited by it and promised to post six of his men to Pollitts Farm, and to alert traffic with descriptions of the three. Cole volunteered to join them. As he and Brunskill rose to leave, Joseph Beck rolled in. He had been celebrating, very enthusiastically, his twenty-two years in the Force, and he was flown with drink. He bore, waveringly, a tray on which three glasses of bitter slopped about. Brunskill took one, mentioning that he couldn't stop, and Jean followed his example. Her job obliged her to drink, whether she wanted to or not, as a token of camaraderie, but she watched the quantities.

When Beck proffered the tray to Cole he was told, 'I have to go, Sergeant.'

Beck's already flushed face turned a deeper red. 'What d'you mean? You refuse a drink with me? Too bloody grand for me, are you, Sergeant Cole?'

Jean said gently, 'Have a half-pint, Gordon.'

Beck was getting into his stride. 'Too bloody high and mighty, you London people, to take a half-pint with a bloody provincial, eh?' He ignored Jean's restraining hand on his arm, and her murmur of 'Take it easy.'

'I *am* taking it easy. Can't he take it easy for five minutes and a half-pint?'

'He'll drink your half-pint, Joseph.'

'Will he? Bloody wonderful, if you'll pardon the expression, ma'am, and any slight lapse for once in my twenty-two bloody years. I think I'm going to tell you a little story, Sergeant Cole.'

The little story which flowed out on a tide of drunken belligerence was a rambling account of the high-handed behaviour of three London Flying Squad men. It embarrassed others in the pub who were forced to listen to it, and caused Cole's face to turn even more pale and set. At the end of it Beck was standing over him, orating between hiccups.

'You lot always have to make the stir, don't you? You can't leave anything to us stupid provincials?'

Jean said, very quietly, 'Now you can stop that, Joseph.'

'One protest in twenty-two years? Don't you think I'm entitled to one? Please give me, ma'am, your answer to that after I've made an urgent call. All right, everybody?' He disappeared under the sign 'Gentlemen'. Jean turned to the frozen-faced Cole.

'I assure you it *is* once in a lifetime. Hard to know whether one rejoices in twenty-two years in the Force, or hates it . . .'

'Yes, ma'am. Will you excuse me?' He followed Beck out, catching him up as he paused before a mirror, a little startled by his own wild appearance. 'You,' said Cole, and pulled him round violently, disregarding his cry of protest. 'If you insult me again, you're in trouble.'

'Hey, take it easy. I wasn't insulting you . . .'

'*You insulted me*. Don't you ever do that again.' He turned his back on the shaken Beck, and went back into the bar.

Jean had been thinking what to say to him. 'I told you it is once in a lifetime.'

'I understood.'

'Maybe you should bend a little, Gordon.'

'I'm not sure about that, ma'am.'

'Why?'

'I get my results by being a little harder than villains.'

'I'm not sure I get the point of that.'

'The point is I catch them, ma'am.'

She eyed him for a moment; cold, inflexible, lonely. 'Are you a happy man, Gordon?' She knew roughly what the answer must be before it came.

'It's what I know, ma'am, and what I do, knowing I do it well, that makes sense of it.'

'You make your entire life the job?'

'Is there another way?'

Thank God, she thought, for me there is. 'There has to be,' she said.

He raised his eyebrows. 'You're talking about degrees of compromise?'

'I'm talking about sanity, Gordon.'

'That may be a luxury for some of us.'

'Are you saying that seriously – that sanity's a luxury?'

He had thought this out. 'Sanity's something we define within ourselves through the purpose of our lives. You compromise that purpose, you can lose the way. Maybe that's what Arthur Roberts did. He should have been too bright to die like that.'

Jean leant forward. 'Tell me the real reason you were a friend of his.'

'A paradox. He grew, over the years, into a worthwhile antagonist. I wanted one day to get him for something really big. Now, by his death, I've been cheated of that.'

'I think that explains quite a lot, Gordon,' she said. 'And I understand it.'

The next time they met was the following morning, in a spot hidden by trees from Pollitts Farm. Parrish, Brunskill and an overhung Beck were holding the fort in Beck's car.

'I talked to the dairy,' she told Cole. 'The milkman says a respectably dressed bloke ordered up the two pints a day, from about four days ago, also some bread, butter, and fresh orange juice. I got wirephotos of Garland and Cantwell – Beck and Parrish are looking at them.'

They saw the approach of the minibus simultaneously, and hastily moved out of sight as it came up the farm drive. There were five men aboard, one of whom Jean recognized as Tony Cantwell. He had a half-empty Scotch bottle in his hand, and it was not difficult to see that all of them had been drinking. So this was a mopping-up operation after the celebratory night. They disembarked, Cantwell produced a key and opened the front door, while the man Jean knew to be Garland picked up the milk bottles. Silently, unobtrusively, Parrish, Brunskill and two plainclothes sergeants joined Jean and Cole. A quick consultation, and he and Jean, the sergeants flanking them, advanced towards the front door of the farm.

In the hall, Cantwell was giving orders to the others.

'Clean up the kitchen table. Charlie, get the Scotch out of the bloody larder – key's on the hook over the fridge. Somebody help me with . . .'

The door burst open, and five shocked faces turned to the invading party. Shock kept them quiet as Brunskill said, 'Anthony Cantwell, Jack James Garland, you're under arrest. Anything you say may be taken down and used in evidence...'

Cantwell shouted to his men, 'Don't kill 'em, just run – beat it – run!'

But as they made for the back door Beck, Parrish and Bentley hurtled through it. In the mêlée that followed the desperate men soon began to get the advantage of the police. A vicious kick overthrew Brunskill, Cantwell wriggled out of the grasp of the plainclothes men, was seized by Bentley, and flung the young constable clean over a hall table, to land heavily on the floor, winded.

'Come on! They're getting away!' Brunskill shouted. But the five were already out of the front door, running headlong in different directions to make pursuit more difficult. Cantwell himself bolted for the minibus, flung himself into it, and was away before anyone could get near him.

Jean looked round for Cole. He was not to be seen. There was no more she could do now, after a valiant attempt to straitjacket one of the villains with his own coat. Then she saw that Garland was heading for the river bank; a certain gamble of hers might be coming off. She hurried in the same direction. Yes, he was making for the moored boat, jumping into it, starting the engine. Jean watched with satisfaction as he untied the painter. The boat began to move out into open water, then swerved abruptly, jerked back by the rope Jean had tied from its bow to a tree.

Startled, thrown off his balance, Garland began to struggle to untie the rope. Jean shouted amiably to him.

'Come in, *Wayfarer II*, your time is up!'

As the swivelling boat hit the bank and Garland toppled out of it into the river, Beck appeared at Jean's side, panting.

'How come... you came directly here, ma'am?'

She smiled. 'I knew you lot would let the two important ones get away.'

They caught up with the minibus in a country lane three miles distant from Pollitts Farm. It was parked, and appeared to be empty. In fact, it was occupied. In the aisle between the seats Cantwell lay face downwards, crying like a child with pain. Cole was kneeling over him, holding one of his arms in a brutal grip. The other lay useless at his side.

Cantwell whimpered. 'You've broken my bloody arm.'

'It really was an accident,' Cole said blandly. 'Now I'm going to break this one if you don't tell me how Arthur died.'

At the station, Cole passed on to Jean and Brunskill the information he had gained.

'Roberts planned the robbery, Cantwell converted the securities in cash, Garland bought the farm. The other three were involved along the line. The deal was to keep the farm six years, sell it, split the money. Roberts wanted more of the split. He threatened them, Garland took out a gun, Roberts made a dive for it and it went off. I'll save details for the report. I'd like to write my report back in London. You'll have it tomorrow, sir.'

Cole politely accepted Jean's offer to drive him to the station. When he had left with Brunskill, Beck requested a word.

'Ma'am, we've had to move Cantwell to hospital. His arm's badly broken. He said Sergeant Cole did it deliberate.'

'Oh? Cole said it was an accident.'

'Did he? Well, I think he's a hard basket. Totally without feeling.'

'Is that right, Joseph?'

'Yes, ma'am.'

On the way to the station, Cole asked Jean to stop at a stonemason's yard, and told her why. She went in with him, through a stone forest of shiny new gravestones, guardian angels, sacred personages and flower urns.

'I've got a friend,' Cole told the stonemason, 'going to be buried.'

'Oh aye, sir.'

'Can you tell me about Burial at Public Expense? Do they provide a headstone up here?'

'No, sir, they do not.'

'What charge for your cheapest stone?'

The man indicated a modest classical vase. 'This item here,

sir, fifty-five pound including VAT, cemetery fee, and fifty letters best engraving.'

'Right.' Cole produced a bundle of fivers from his wallet and wrote on the notepad the man provided. The mason read out what he had written.

'*Arthur S. Roberts, born 1919, died 1980*. You got plenty more letters to write a quote, like *Nearer my God to Thee*, or *Rest in peace*.'

Cole took back the pad. '*Arthur S. Roberts, born 1919, died 1980*. No. No, there's not a lot else you could say about him.'

Parked by the railway station, hearing the departure of the train carrying Cole south, she thought back to her conversation with him in the pub, and what he had said. 'A little harder than villains . . . is there another way? . . . cheated by his death . . .' Was that all there was to Gordon Cole?

She knew now that it was not.

chapter six

'I'm sorry, dear, I can't possibly come over tomorrow,' said the telephone. 'Daddy's got a round to play off with Colonel Foster, and it's my bridge afternoon.'

'But, Mother . . . I've simply no one else to ask. I don't know any of the neighbours yet, and in any case I don't much want to let the key out of my hands.'

'I'm sure you can manage somehow, dear. You always do.' The Lancashire undertones in the voice of Jean's mother were pronounced on the telephone, managing to convey what Jean well knew were her feelings – that a daughter who did anything so unusual and unsuitable as running a police station was quite outside the ordinary rules of life. With only one daughter to three sons, Mrs Haywood had felt herself entitled to a daughter who would be a real companion to her and enjoy the same social pleasures, instead of which she had turned out virtually another boy. Not that Jean was unfeminine; indeed, a lot of men thought her very attractive, and she liked nice clothes and things as much as any other girl. And of course Mrs Haywood was proud of her, and talked much of her important status. Only it was not the same, quite, as having the sort of daughter she had meant to have.

'Can't Tom stand in for you?' she asked. 'He must have a lot more time now that he's only doing this Social Services job. I mean, it's not like being at Speke.'

'It's not a case of "only", Mother. The job's absolutely full-time, what with home visits and court appearances and all the rest of it . . .' Jean stopped, aware that no amount of talking on her part would convince her mother that Tom had not somehow mislaid his nice job as a design engineer through sheer carelessness, or that what he was doing now was not some kind of vague charity work. She liked her son-in-law – it was impossible not to – but if only Jean had married a really strong, forceful man who would have made her settle down to be a wife with nice home interests . . .

Tom himself shook his head at Jean, smiling. He could hear clearly what the voice in Southport was saying.

'All right, Mother,' Jean said with finality. 'Never mind. I expect it will work out. Yes, of course come over and see the house – when we're in it. It'll be a nice drive over the moors for you. Goodbye.'

She hung up. 'So much for relations!'

'Did you really think she'd come over?'

'I don't suppose I did. Waste of time talking. Why don't we all have masses of nice maiden aunts, like the Victorians, always willing to oblige?'

Tom lit his pipe. There was really no answer. Jean was finding out, painfully, the difference between a man and a woman holding the same position with, ostensibly, the same privileges. Now that the long weeks of solicitors' to-ing and fro-ing were over, and contracts exchanged, the new house was theirs. But before they could move into it there were things to be done. The carpets from the old house that fitted the new rooms had already been taken up ready for laying before the furniture went in, and a new sitting-room carpet was on order. A new gas cooker was to be fitted in the kitchen; the power points had proved to be too few, and someone from the Electricity Board was coming to add to them. The single telephone in the new house proved, on inspection, to be grimy and battered. In any case Jean needed an extension in the bedroom, which the Telephone Manager had promised should be fitted in the minimum time. Any request from the lady Inspector was treated very seriously.

None of which allowed for the fact that Jean's time belonged to the Force, not to her. That morning she had arranged to be an hour late on duty to let in the electrician. Promptly at 8.45 she had arrived, opened up, and waited. At 9.15, when he was a quarter of an hour late, she had telephoned.

'No, he didn't come in this morning,' a voice told her. 'Had to go off yesterday afternoon to take his wife to the hospital.'

'Well, can't you send someone else?'

'I will if anyone's free, dear, but they're all out on other jobs, far as I know.'

'I can wait until a quarter to ten. Can you telephone whoever was supposed to be coming and get him here quickly?'

The voice seemed to think this a very unusual proceeding, but eventually said that it would try.

At ten minutes to ten Jean left. Nobody had arrived.

Sergeant Parrish noted her ruffled air, and attempted to cheer her up.

'There's a customer in Number Three.'

'Oh? Why wasn't I told before?'

'Only brought in this morning, seven-thirty. I tried to phone you, ma'am, but there was no answer.'

'There wouldn't be. I was . . . oh, never mind. What seems to be the matter with him – if it is a him?'

'It is, and it looks like meths. The doctor's down there now. Bit of an untidy state he was in,' Parrish added delicately. Jean took the implication; a mess in the immaculate cells that were the pride of her heart.

'Cup of tea?' Parrish suggested.

'Please, George. And tell Roland not to fall over with it this time.'

She said to Tom, that evening, 'I wouldn't have minded so much if I hadn't called in at the house on my way back tonight, and found this.' The printed slip that had been stuck in the letter-box said: *Our representative called today as arranged but could obtain no answer. Please telephone for a further appointment.*

'I'd already telephoned, of course, to find out what the matter was, but nobody seemed to know anything. All they could say was that he couldn't possibly do the job until Friday. Friday, when I'm in City all morning, and you're in court.' Tom spent his time during this period of learning the job going round with Senior Officers.

'And your mother won't play. When's moving day again?'

'Thursday week.'

Tom stroked Blackie, who had jumped on his lap, from head to tail. 'At this rate we'll be in the old home another year or two.'

'A lot of use *he* is,' Jean said, eyeing the cat. 'Settling him in's going to be a job in itself, and if he thinks I'm staying to hold his paw he can think again.'

A respectful telephone message to the Station next morning informed Jean that, if convenient, an engineer would attend that afternoon at 4.30 to install the new instruments. She checked her diary and found that she could get away, if nothing came up. At 4.20 Beck appeared.

'What is it, Joseph?'

'Just wanted a word, ma'am. About the leave rota. I'd like to nip over to Ireland for the kid's school holidays, and it looks on paper as if . . .'

'I'm very sorry, Joseph, I can't discuss it just now. I've got to be somewhere in ten minutes. Tomorrow, first thing?'

She knew that he would not actually look at her desk calendar or at the clock, but that they would be in the forefront of his mind. 'I'm moving house next week and there are things to do,' she said, then wished she hadn't offered the apologia. His look said, quite plainly, Bloody women. This is what comes of putting them in charge. And he was disappointed, unable to finalize his leave there and then. He was divorced, and it had been a bitter divorce. His ex-wife had gone back to her native Ireland, taking their eight-year-old daughter, whom he adored. It mattered a lot to Beck to get time to fly over and see the little girl.

As her Mini rounded the corner of the avenue she saw the telephone van at the gate, and the engineer getting into it. She accelerated and pulled up in front of him.

'Hey!' she called. 'Where do you think you're going?'

He got out of the car and came up to her, a handsome boy with a cheerful grin. 'This your place, love? Thought you wasn't in.'

'I wasn't. I arranged to meet you here at four-thirty. It's now exactly four-thirty-one.' She displayed her large digital watch, which he regarded with admiration.

'That's a right 'un, that is.' As she left the car he took in the fact of her uniform, and whistled, putting his hands up in mock fear.

'Okay, I'll come quietly. They didn't tell me they was puttin' the fuzz on me.'

'No?' Jean locked her car, thinking, If he calls me a fair cop I'll kill him. She was aware of his admiring stare taking in her trim uniform, the slim waist accentuated by the belt, the smart chequered cap that she knew suited her. If he got fresh in the house she would give him the usual treatment. But he only said, 'The fuzz don't lock their cars on telly.'

'Don't they? They should. It's a bad example to the public.'

'Aye, it is. Maybe it's because they've not the time. Time costs money, on telly, that's what you read in t'papers.'

In the house he proved to be brisk and efficient at his job, to her relief, fitting the two smart cream handsets he had brought with practised speed, at the same time singing a pop tune very loudly. At least he hadn't brought a transistor. The bedroom instrument installed, he came clattering down the uncarpeted stairs.

'That's it, then. Okay, love?'

'Okay. Thanks.' She was not in the habit of tipping unnecessarily, but she was so grateful that something had gone right at last. He seemed pleased and surprised, and went off singing even louder.

Good, it was only just after five o'clock. Time to go back and put in another hour's work. As she was going out of the gate a woman emerged from the house next door, so promptly that she must have been watching. She was small, middle-aged, with an anxious placatory smile; intuition told Jean that she was lonely.

'Oh, excuse me – I just happened to see you – and I wondered . . . I've noticed you calling in, and I thought – I mean, you must be very busy . . .'

'Yes, I am, rather.' Jean smiled, hoping that her neighbour was not all set for a long cosy chat.

'Oh, you must be, yes. I thought, if it would help – to let me have your key – I could let workmen in for you, instead of you having to be here . . . but of course you might not like that . . .' She sounded despondent at the thought.

'Well, that's very kind of you.' Jean was thinking rapidly. It would be a solution, and the woman was obviously respectable. Jean wouldn't have put it past her, on first judgement, to have ideas about slipping in and having a good look round, but if she did it wouldn't matter, there was nothing in the place.

'I think it might be a great help,' she said. 'If I could leave it with you now – I could arrange for the electrician to come early on Friday morning. He'll be here a fair time, so I'll ask him to drop it through your letterbox when he goes.'

'Oh, that will be *quite* all right. It's Fairweather. Mrs Fairweather. I'm so pleased you're going to be living next door, I must say. I'm alone so much, you know, my hubby doesn't get in till after seven, and I shall feel so much more protected, with you there . . .'

Jean smiled. 'I can't guarantee protection, I'm afraid. But you'll probably feel better with someone living next door.'

'Oh yes! Six months it's been empty, not nice at all.' Mrs Fairweather eyed the uniform. 'Very smart, your costume, isn't it. You must have such an interesting job. Do you do just the same sort of work as the men?'

The nice cosy chat was evidently materializing. Jean looked at her watch, expressed surprise at the time, and left after handing over the key. Mrs Fairweather gazed wistfully after her.

Thursday began frantically. In the middle of what should have been a morning of paperwork Jean was called out.

'Message from Hanley Lane,' Beck said. 'They can't shift the old man.'

'Not old Mr Carter? I thought that was all fixed.'

'Not now it isn't. Seems he went back on it when the van turned up this morning – said he wasn't getting out after all.'

'Oh no.' Old Mr Carter had been a problem ever since plans for a projected motorway extension had been finalized. His cottage, one of several old houses straggling along Hanley Lane, stood in the way of it, and a compulsory purchase order had been served on all the cottagers, who had obeyed it, with varying degrees of protest and grumbling. But Mr Carter had simply refused to accept the position. He was not, he said, leaving. Then, to everyone's relief, he capitulated – only to go back on his word, it seemed.

'Blast,' Jean said. 'I suppose I'll have to go and talk to him.'

The two young ones, Bentley and Davies, went with her. Hanley Lane was on the far outskirts of Hartley. Once it had been country, with a moorland air to it, but now it was characterless, a disused and almost deserted place. The road had never been made up; pools of muddy rainwater stood between its ruts, and cinders had been thrown down at some time in an attempt to level its surface. The cottages were neither particularly old nor attractive, belonging to the period of Queen Victoria's Diamond Jubilee; square brick boxes with built-out porches and untended gardens in front. One had a low brick wall instead of a fence, on which somebody had long ago chalked *Stones Rule OK.*

Jean surveyed the last in the row, old Carter's. A removal van stood in front, three men lounging outside it, smoking.

'Not exactly roses round the door.'

'It's a mess,' Davies said. 'Why'd anyone want to hang on to a place like that?'

'People have different ideas of what makes a home, and Carter's seem to be pretty strong.'

'I could go and chat him up, ma'am,' Bentley said eagerly. 'I'm supposed to be good with old folk.'

'Thank you, Roland. But I'll have a go myself.' She got out and approached the removal men.

'Old chap won't even talk to us,' the foreman told her. 'Shouted round the door that he wasn't budging and we might as well go away. He's upstairs now – every now and then he looks out. Wasting our time, this is.'

'How long have you been here?'

'Best part of two hours.'

'All right. I'll see what I can do.' She entered the shabby, overgrown little front garden and looked up. From one of the bedroom windows someone was peering down. She shouted, 'Mr Carter?' Fortunately it was a still morning – voices would carry, unless the old man turned out to be deaf.

After two more vain appeals, she picked up a pebble and threw it accurately up at the window. This time the sash was pushed up and Carter's head appeared. It was quite bald, and he hadn't shaved for some days.

'Don't you go throwing stones at my windows!' he shouted. 'I'll have the law on you.'

'I *am* the law, Mr Carter.'

'You? You're nowt but a dressed-up wench.'

'Don't shut the window, Mr Carter. I'm Inspector Darblay, in charge of Hartley Section. What's all this about you refusing to leave?'

He was leaning out of the window now, arms folded on the sill, apparently prepared to enjoy himself. Good, we'll be able to talk, thought Jean.

'It's what you said,' he answered. 'I refuse to leave. This is my house, and I'm stopping here.'

'It isn't your house any more, Mr Carter. It belongs to the district authorities, by compulsory purchase.'

'They've purchased nowt! Kept sending me letters, but I wouldn't sign. This was my dad's house and I were born here, and I'll not be shifted.'

Jean tried another tactic. 'Can I come in, please, Mr Carter? I think we ought to have a talk, instead of shouting like this. And these removal chaps would be very glad of a cup of tea.'

'They'll get no tea out of me, I'm telling you.'

'Please.' She smiled up at him. Womanly wiles were out, in her job, but there was no harm in using a little charm. It worked. After a moment he said, 'Aye, well. *You* can come in, if you like.'

The interior of the cottage was no more picturesque than the outside. The one living-room was filled with furniture neither antique nor modern, and its air was fusty. She guessed that Mr Carter employed no cleaner and did very little cleaning himself. There were large, fading family photographs on the walls and mantelpiece, a Cornish pixie mascot, some assorted china in a glass-fronted cabinet, a miniature harmonium. On the hearthrug, obviously made by inexpert or crippled hands (why should the image of a cripple come into her mind?) lay the model of a small dog. She looked at it closer, and saw that it had only one eye, and that whole patches of its fur were missing. Realization dawned on her that the dog was dead, stuffed.

Mr Carter had been fiddling about with tea things in the lean-to kitchen. Coming back with a clumsily laid tray, he saw her looking at the gruesome relic.

'That's our Toby. Mother thought t'world of him. She couldn't get out, towards the end, wi' her trouble. So when he went, I had him done for her.'

Drinking the strong, over-sugared tea, Jean looked around at the litter of objects. Things nobody would give house-room to, things that would go for a song in job-lots at a sale: things that spoke of people's lives, when the people themselves were gone.

She was surprised to find the old man's watery eyes on her, even more surprised by his words, seeming to echo her thoughts.

'Aye, it's a home. Not sort a lass like you'd want, I expect. You've got a home of your own, haven't you?'

'Yes,' she said, thinking, Have I, though? That empty place with only a couple of new telephones in it to say anything about me, about the way I like things; is that a home, yet?

'Seventy-seven year I've lived here. I can't give it up now, can I? I thowt you looked a sensible lass, as'd see it my way.'

Jean put down her cup. 'I do see it your way, Mr Carter. I know this place means a lot to you. Everything, perhaps. If I'd lived here as long as you I expect I'd feel the same. But a home's not bricks and mortar, is it? This place has been built a long time – best part of a hundred years. It's not had much done to it recently – the roof's defective and you've got damp in the walls, and some dry rot by the smell of it.'

His face had darkened again; he was disappointed in her.

'What's that supposed to mean?'

'This house wants a lot of money spending on it. I don't suppose you'd feel like doing that? If you stayed here everything would get worse, and you'd be uncomfortable and perhaps ill. We're not asking you to give up your home, Mr Carter – only the outside walls. There's a nice flat waiting for you in Folds Road, in a new development there. Haven't you been to see it?'

'Nay.'

'Well, I know those flats well, and they're grand. Plenty of room, enough for all your things. You could take every single thing you've got here.' She didn't add that there would be somebody in residence at Folds Road to look in on him and make sure he was all right, somebody to call on in an emergency, a warden and a nurse, for Folds Road was 'sheltered housing'. It was just the sort of detail to put off this independent, solitary old man. Sensing a wavering in him, she said, 'And, whether you've signed anything or not, they won't let you stay here. This house is coming down, like the others, and neither you nor I can stop it. Nothing can, now, except an Act of God. So hadn't you better make up your mind to go? Come on – be a good lad.'

He said nothing, but got up stiffly and hobbled into the kitchen. She heard him clattering about, and sat quiet, waiting. It was a full two minutes before he came back. He looked even older, broken, the fight gone out of him.

'All right,' he said. 'When do I go?'

She put an arm round his shoulder. 'Don't you worry. You stay here for a minute and I'll tell those lads to make a good quick job of it. Have you got a drop of spirits in the house?'

He looked defensive. 'Medicinal purposes.'

'Of course.' It always was medicinal purposes. 'Where is it, love?'

He pointed to a corner cupboard. There was a half-bottle, barely touched, of a good brand of Scotch. She poured a generous but not unwise measure into his teacup, and watched him drink before she went out to the removal men and the waiting Escort. To the foreman she said, 'Okay now. Make it quick. We'll get him out of the way,' and to the two constables, 'What's a quiet place near here for a coffee, pie and chips, that sort of thing?'

'Ted's Cafe,' Davies said. 'Are we going for a bit of nosh, then?'

'We're taking Mr Carter for a bite to eat while they're shifting his stuff. It'll keep his mind off things.'

Bentley looked admiringly at her. 'You're a miracle-worker, ma'am.'

'No, I've only got a bit more common sense than some of the folk that's been talking to him.'

Old Carter seemed not to realize that he was virtually being abducted. The whisky had blurred reality for him. In the police car he looked about him vaguely, and Jean wondered if he had been in many cars in all his life. Ted's Cafe was empty of customers. The four of them sat down and Jean ordered coffee for all of them and whatever the boys wanted. Carter ate mechanically, but with such readiness that Jean was sure he had not eaten at all recently. Soon she noticed that he and Bentley were talking, young Roland making pleasantries that were meaningless but comprehensible to the old man. He seemed to say the right things quite without effort; he was happily unselfconscious, completely natural, irresistibly kind and open. So he had been right, he was good with old folk.

She dropped out of the conversation, then said quietly to Davies, 'Can you manage him at Folds Road, do you think?'

'Sure we can.'

'Then I'll leave you two there. You can walk back to the nick, can't you?'

At the entrance to the flats the two boys helped old Carter out of the car and, one on each side, up the few steps to the hallway. He turned and looked back at her with the beginnings of a watery smile, then turned away, forgetting, as Bentley distracted his attention.

He would be all right. Or as all right as he would ever be. She wondered if the embalmed Toby would survive the journey in the removal van.

Jean's day ended at seven in the evening. Everything she had not expected to happen had happened. She looked forward to a peaceful meal with Tom, a look at television, early bed.

Tom was in the kitchen, reheating the casserole she had left. He looked unhappy and strained. She kissed him, knowing better than to ask what was the matter. That was for unwinding-time.

'Go on,' she said, 'ask me if I've had a hard day at the office, and I'll give you a short sharp answer.'

He didn't smile. 'Jean – before you go in – we've got a visitor.'

'*Visitor?* Who on earth—?'

'It's your mother.'

'Hell's teeth! Oh, no. I don't believe it.'

But Mrs Haywood was there, reclining comfortably on the couch, reading a magazine. She was immaculate in the kind of tailored yet feminine clothes that suited her neat plump figure; her hair, rinsed to the colour of dark honey, shone with care; a cluster of diamonds nestled on her manicured hand.

'Well, Jean. It was such a nice day, I thought I'd pop over after all and give you a surprise.'

'You did that all right, Mother. But why "after all"?'

'The electrician, of course, dear! You can't have forgotten you asked me?'

Jean sat down heavily, understanding why despairing people in novels clutch their hair. 'But that was the other day, Mother, and I've rearranged it all. The woman next door has the key to let him in. You should have phoned – let me know, and saved yourself all this trouble . . .'

'Oh, it was no trouble, dear. I quite enjoyed the drive. The heather's out, lovely. And now tomorrow I can see your new little house after all, and perhaps we can do some shopping afterwards, and have lunch. Not that I think all that much of the Hartley shops, but there's a new Joneses, isn't there, and I expect they've got their own restaurant, their stores always do. You can try the new car out, see what you think of it. I do hope it's all right standing out in the road, but Tom says it will be, and how nice for you having a garage of your own at the new house . . .'

'Mother. I'm very sorry, I don't think you understand. I've got to work – I'm in City all morning, and probably half the afternoon.'

It took Jean most of suppertime to convince her mother that police business actually took priority over shopping, but in the end Mrs Haywood found herself quite looking forward to a gentle potter round on her own. Then there was the matter of putting her up, in a guest-room from which the carpet had already been removed, and the bare boards stacked with packaged books, ornaments and bedding. The refurbishing of it took so long that it passed the early bedtime Jean had hoped for, and while she and Tom were working on it Mrs Haywood took the opportunity to have a bath, thereby using up all the hot water. At the door of her room, warm and sweet-smelling, she patted Jean's cheek.

'You're too thin, dear. Why do you let them work you so hard? Don't bother about me in the morning, now – I'll just have a nice egg on toast up here, so as not to get in your way downstairs . . .'

'God!' Jean said to Tom downstairs. 'You can be as draconian as all get out with your mates, but relations . . . especially when they mean well . . . what the hell can you do?'

He was not answering lightly, not being his usual understanding self. 'What is it?' she asked.

He shook his head. 'I don't want to talk about it. It was . . . something, a case I went on with the Senior Officer. I've never seen anything like it.' He shuddered.

'Kids?' she asked quietly, knowing what hit Tom most.

'A kid. Teenage stepfather, not married to the mother . . . said he lost his temper once, but it was worse than that . . .' His voice died away.

'We'll be coming in on it, then. Think you got on to it in time?'

'I hope so. I don't know. Jean, I don't think I've picked the right job.'

'Give it time, love. Give it time.'

Jean lay awake, the events of the day going through her mind. The old house, feeling strange and unfriendly now that they were deserting it. The new one, echoingly empty, so much trouble, as much bother as a baby. Mr Carter and his clutter of beloved, fusty trash, in a decaying cottage. A flat, or a house, somewhere in Hartley, with cruelty in it enough to shock the heart out of Tom.

Homes . . . houses . . . when is a house a home, or not a home?

She was asleep.

chapter seven

'The nick's going to be like a rest cure after this,' Jean said, surveying her new kitchen. The week's leave she had taken for the removal had been packed with incident, most of it the sort she could have done without. Now everything had gone quiet again.

The new carpet for the living-room had been bought at the expense of the upstairs floors, which were covered only with scatter-rugs. The kitchen looked bare and was sadly deficient in working surfaces without the new units they couldn't afford to buy. Tom, with his designer's eye, knew exactly what was wanted and where it should go, but paying for costly wood and elaborate fittings was another matter.

'Anyway,' he said, 'we can always look out of the window. The garden's coming on nicely. Plenty of roses still out, and some nice dahlias. Why don't you pick some, then you won't notice the gaps so much?'

'Nice idea, but do you know what time it is? What do you bet the car won't start? That's all I need.'

The Mini, possibly appreciative of its new garage home, graciously behaved itself. Monday morning, here we go . . .

In a Hartley backstreet someone else was contemplating a car. Johnny Duffield was nine years old, a thin sharp-faced creature like a whippet puppy. He looked as if nobody cared for him, which in fact was the case. His eyes, like his quicksilver legs, were never still except when they rested on something he coveted – something to steal. This morning it was an invalid car.

The Invacar was a smart three-wheeler of blue fibreglass, and it was parked in the street because its owner, old Mr Stainley, had nowhere else to keep it. Johnny was pleased to see that he had been trusting enough not to lock the windows. After a swift look up and down the street he opened a window and got in. In his pocket was a coil of electric wire. He used it to cut out the starter switch. Johnny knew all about cars. The engine leapt into life.

Mr Stainley heard it and knew it for what it was. He propelled his wheelchair to the window just in time to see the car start, and Johnny's face at the wheel. Then it moved off smoothly down the street and out of sight.

Its owner cursed loudly and at length on his way to the telephone. 'Police,' he shouted into it. 'Police, and bloody quick!'

The car thief was already speeding along a dual carriageway on the edge of the town. He was excited, thrilled, revelling in his adventure, tearing up the yards and miles. He was a racing driver, a proper daredevil, he was the king of the road, a helmeted god in a flash arrow of a car, latest model, the pride of Brands Hatch, the one the crowds pointed to at Le Mans, he was flying, soaring – he was the guy on the motorbike in the film.

The rear mirror showed him a police car tailing him, flashing its lights, its gong going. In a moment it would be level with him. He slammed on the brakes, and as the car halted he leapt out and began to run. He ran very fast, like a human hare, but the policeman's legs were longer than his, and before he could get out of reach he was cornered and held in a strong grip.

'All right,' said Jean, when Parrish broke the news of the latest culprit. 'Nine years old, with a history.'

'About as long as Irish history, give or take a bit. Ask Sergeant Beck, he'll tell you, he knows the kid.'

'Where is he?'

'Cells.'

She frowned. 'I don't like kids in the cells.'

'This one has to go in cells.'

'Why?'

''Cause nothing can contain him except a six-inch steel door. That's Johnny Duffield.'

'I don't believe it. You're joking.'

'I wish I was,' said Beck.

Jean sat back in her chair. 'Well, go on, tell me all.'

'He first came to our notice three years ago—'

She interrupted. 'Not the "came to our notice" stuff, Sergeant – just the facts.'

Beck didn't like being interrupted, and knew he mustn't show it. After the very slightest pause of reproof he went on. 'He's nearly nine. His father's an invalid. Mother's dead – died when he was six. His first shoplifting offences date from his sixth year.'

'Go on.'

'The kid was placed in two special schools, but he kept running away, whatever they did to keep him in. He's back now in council care. He's run away four times this year, for periods averaging a month. By my guess, he lives rough about four months of the year.'

'Rough? How rough?'

'Around the place – on the moor, in old buildings, factories, that sort of thing – shoplifts for food and pocket-money.'

'And you say he's nine years old?'

'More like eight and three-quarters,' Beck said.

She sighed. 'When I came to this job I asked for a rundown on local villains. You didn't include this one!'

'Well, he's not exactly a major criminal, ma'am. He runs away from care. We find him living rough. We grab him, pull him in, really to find out what state he's in. Give him a good wash, a square meal, and return him to council care, where he runs away again.'

'And nothing else is done?'

'No,' Beck answered with an air that suggested he was personally being accused of not doing more for the boy.

'Hold on a minute. A nine-year-old living half his year rough. Sergeant, this is England, 1980. It isn't kids on the streets of wartime Naples.'

'Well,' he said with some satisfaction, 'you see if you can improve on our response to this situation, ma'am.'

'I bloody well hope I do improve on it. All right, let's go down.'

Johnny Duffield was lounging on the bench of his cell, giving a convincing impression of someone completely relaxed and at home, his hands in his pockets. They stayed there as Jean and Beck entered. Beck slammed the heavy door behind them, and Jean fancied she saw a faint tremor pass through the boy. As he seemed unprepared to start the conversation, she said, 'I'm Inspector Darblay.'

He surveyed her coolly. 'A girl?'

'A girl.' If Sergeant Beck thought this funny, his expression gave no sign of it. 'Why did you steal that invalid car?'

'I didn't.'

'What d'you mean, you didn't?'

'I just didn't.'

'You were seen driving the car and detained by uniformed Traffic Patrol.'

'No, I wasn't,' came the mechanical response.

'Yes, you were.' The exchanges were beginning to sound very silly, but one couldn't let the child's flat denials go unchallenged. Beck explained, 'This is what you call his house style, ma'am – he always denies everything.'

'Is that right?' Jean asked Johnny, who predictably replied, 'No.'

She surveyed him, staring at her with lacklustre eyes, scrawny, unprepossessing. 'Sergeant Beck here tells me you're well known around these parts.' Ignoring his automatic 'I'm not', she went on, 'He tells me you're in the habit of running away from care, living rough, shoplifting. Can you tell me, please, have you any complaints about the council care home, St Edward's House?'

No answer, only the stare. Then, with an effort, he said, 'It's daft.'

'What's daft?'

'The grown-ups there are daft.'

'Why are they daft?'

He shrugged. 'Because they are.'

'Daft about what?'

'Everything.'

Jean's patience was running out. 'Like what?'

'Everything.'

'Well,' she said briskly, 'this isn't getting us anywhere, is it? You've stolen a car.'

'I have not.'

'So we'll have to take you to court, won't we?'

'No, you won't.'

'Why won't we?'

'There's no damage to t'car. It's not worth your bloody while to take me to court.'

Beck put in, 'He's learnt a few tricks in his time, ma'am.'

'So it seems.' To Johnny she said, 'What will you do if we return you to St Edward's House? Will you run away again?'

The same flat answer. 'No.'

'That's a fib, isn't it,' Beck said.

'Fib's a bloody soft word.'

Beck had been through it all before. 'We'd better ask him when he last ate, ma'am.'

This time a negative was impossible, even to Johnny. He admitted that his last meal had been the previous night.

'We usually get him some fish and chips if he's hungry, ma'am.' Beck volunteered.

Johnny produced a whole sentence. 'But this time don't give 'em over in newspaper. I want 'em on a plate with a knife and fork.'

'Anything else you want?' Jean inquired, aware that sarcasm would be lost on Johnny. His answer surprised her.

'A lawyer.'

'But we haven't charged you with anything yet!'

'If I'm not arrested, what am I doin' in here?'

Jean had the last word from the door. 'You're waiting for fish and chips on a plate with a knife and fork.'

As the door shut Johnny put his tongue out at it.

Back in the office she said to Beck, 'I'll have to think this one out carefully – there's a few possible pitfalls.'

'You can say that again, ma'am,' replied Beck heavily. Where Johnny Duffield was concerned he could see nothing but pitfalls.

She picked up the telephone and asked to be put through to Tom at Social Services. Then she asked Beck, 'Any more bad news?'

'Bill Cowley's in the Interview Room. So-called Crime

Reporter on the local paper. Local expert on Real Ale and how to consume it.'

'Oh, yes, I think I met him. Bring him in – I imagine he's not come to talk about Real Ale. After that I want a word with St Edward's House, then we'll go and visit Mr Stainley and Duffield Senior.'

Beck looked disapproving. Trust her to jump the gun. 'Before seeing Duffield Senior we should inform Social Services of any intended investigation.'

'That's what I'm doing – I'm telling my old man.'

'With respect, ma'am, we have to be a little more formal – approach the Senior Officer.' One of these days he would catch her on a point of protocol. This, however, was not the time. She came back at him:

'*With respect*, Sergeant Beck, I'm not too interested in demarcation discussions. I've got a nine-year-old felon down below in my cells, and that's my exclusive responsibility. Plus he has a history that shows an inordinate lack of control by the Social Services. So if you don't mind, I'm going to try and sort it out.'

Beck had no answer to this. 'I'll get Mr Cowley,' he said.

Bill Cowley was a fair representative of one type of local reporter. Middle-aged, he had grown up with his paper, which so far as he was concerned was more important than the national press. He took his job utterly seriously, fancied his own nose for a story, and was confident, even brash, in his approach to anybody who might furnish him with one. His complexion and figure gave ample testimony to his devotion to Real Ale. Jean remembered him well as soon as he came through the door; he was not going to be her favourite visitor, but she smiled and remarked that they had met.

'Yes, indeed,' he boomed, sitting down on a chair which disappeared beneath him. 'Yes, indeed, at the King Harold. How long you been here now, couple of months? Time for a nice little article in my paper, Inspector ma'am – how you've settled in and how the men are reacting to a woman at the helm, that sort of thing.'

He was going to need firm handling. 'I'm pretty busy this morning, so if you could be brief . . .'

Undaunted, he suggested, 'I could meet you at the George, lunchtime.'

'No, Mr Cowley. Can I have your inquiry?'

'Yes, Inspector. In a nutshell, it's this. It's that IRA arms cache that was found in Halifax, two days back.'

'Yes? I read something in the paper.'

Cowley set his hands on his massive thighs. 'So did I, Inspector, the statement of the Anti-Terrorist Squad. Did you see that?'

'No.'

'Head of Anti-Terrorist Squad stated that information in their possession suggested that the Halifax find was the third cache of six major arms dumps in the area. When pressed to reveal when the next discoveries would be made, he said – and I think you know this – the Anti-Terrorist Squad was surveillancing a cache which like Halifax was situated tactically midway between major motorways, and might well in fact turn out to be the operational headquarters for the Provos in England. Well, Inspector?'

'Well what?'

He laughed. 'Come now, Inspector. Hartley's almost midway between M6 and M1, and on direct route A646 to Halifax.'

Jean sighed audibly. 'What are you saying, Mr Cowley?'

'The biggest story of the decade, dear! And all I'm asking you to do is to tip me the nod, pick up the phone and give me a ring when the Anti-Terrorist Squad move in to make those arrests – no doubt backed by the local police.'

She leaned forward. 'You're wrong, Mr Cowley. There is, to my knowledge, no interest by the Anti-Terrorist Squad in this area – and not a whisper of anything involving the Provisional IRA. That's the truth.'

'Yes, well, is it?' He was used to bullying females, but this one wasn't responding. 'What I'm going to do is leave telephone numbers with your desk sergeant where I can be got day and night. And I'll leave it on your conscience about whether you feel an obligation to your local press.'

With relief she saw his bulky form bounce out of her office, as the telephone rang to connect her with Tom.

Johnny Duffield was led from his cell to the Interview Room, where Jean had arranged for his lunch to be served. He looked apprehensively round the stark, brightly lit room.

'What's this, then? I don't want to eat here. I usually eat with desk sergeant,' he protested.

Beck gave him a push. 'We're not running a restaurant. Get in there.'

Johnny backed. 'No! It's got no windows. You're going to lock me in.'

'We're not,' Parrish assured him, but Johnny, showing emotion for once, repeated, 'It's got no bloody windows!' Then, before they could stop him, he was off and away, down the long corridor and out through the door into the street, leaving behind him two flustered, panting sergeants and a plateful of fish and chips scattered on the floor.

They chased him, Beck, Parrish and Bentley, until they could run no longer and his flying figure had disappeared among undergrowth where the town ended and the moor began, a no-man's-land. They stopped, breathless, and looked at each other. They wouldn't catch up with Johnny, even with cars, in such territory. Not looking forward to their encounter with their Inspector, they returned to the station.

'I don't bloody well believe it,' Jean told them. 'You let a nine-year-old get away from you . . .' She turned from the abashed sergeants to dictate Johnny's description into her hand-mike. 'John David Duffield, aged nine, wearing navy blue anorak, yellow sleeve inserts, white T-shirt, short pants, and gym-type running shoes which he's currently putting to very good use.'

Beck, still sore from her criticism, went with her to see Johnny's father. Duffield Senior was older than a father of a nine-year-old might be expected to be. He looked, and was, a disappointed man. Disappointed with life, with his son, everything. His legs were useless to him, having been crushed in an accident at work, and he propelled himself about on metal walking-sticks. The place he lived in was small, mean and cheerless, just two rooms, the living-room also a work-room, with a knitting machine and boxes of knits in evidence. Finishing was the only kind of work he was fit for now.

Gloomily he showed them in. 'Make yourselves at home, as usual. What is it?'

'It's Johnny,' Jean said.

'Aye, it's always Johnny. What's it about Johnny now?'

'He's in trouble.'

'He's in council care. If he's in trouble, they're in trouble. They're supposed to look after him.'

'He stole a car,' Beck said. 'We caught him. He escaped from our custody. We're looking for some ideas on where he might have gone.'

'Well. He finds himself a derelict building, or makes himself a hut on the moor, and that's it.'

'Do you think he can survive out there?' Jean asked. 'It's September – it's getting cold at night.'

Duffield snapped back at her, ''Course he survives out there. I've heard of you – you're the new woman copper. Well, lass, two years ago your lads used to be in and out of this room three, maybe four times a month. Asking me, a bloody cripple, what I was doing about him. Well, I've belted him, talked to him, tried everything and nothing works. And you know that nothing bloody works, or you wouldn't be here.'

Jean knew that there was no use in arguing with the man, and that there was probably very little to be got out of him. Beck was asking if Duffield knew anyone with an invalid car on which Johnny might have learnt to wire-tap the ignition. Duffield smiled sourly.

'They learn everything they know at that council care place, St Edward's House. It's a wonderful education and upbringing.'

'And you're not worried about Johnny living rough out there? He's only nine. What d'you think he's going to grow up into?'

'A first-class tearaway,' Johnny's father answered calmly.

'Doesn't that worry you?'

'There's very little worries me any more, lass. Can I ask what you're asking me these questions for?'

'I came to see how badly disabled you were. You obviously cope well. You can work, and you're not immobile. I think a boy like that should be with his dad.'

Duffield met her eyes stonily. 'Well, I couldn't handle it.'

Beck was acutely embarrassed to hear her ask, 'Don't you love your son at all?' It was not a question he would have come out with in a thousand years.

'No,' said Duffield.

'Then we'd better get on and do your job for you.'

'Aye, you had. And by the way, he doesn't love me. He never has. Off you go.'

A message awaited them at the station. Johnny had once again pounced on Mr Stainley's Invacar, and this time another lad was with him. Mr Stainley was, not surprisingly, furious, and told them so when they called on him. He was a very angry old man indeed.

'Stealing my bloody car once – oh aye, that's within realms of reason, but then to come back and bung it off twice . . . Is this bloody world gone mad?'

'We're very sorry for this,' Jean told him.

'Oh, are you? Well, you bloody understand this. That car is my survival, or not, as the case may be. I need that car to shop for me food, to get me pills from the chemist, and for emergencies. I got a dicky heart, you know. Last time there was an emergency, I phoned ambulance – ambulance on strike. If I hadn't had that car and staggered into it, and got to hospital, I'd be pushing up moorwort now. Much you care.'

He continued in the same vein until they left. Beck was feeling very downcast. It was bad enough that he should have been unable to stop the little devil getting away, but that it should happen again . . . Jean said no more about his part in the escape, but he was uncomfortably conscious that she was mindful of it. A personal capture of Johnny Duffield would, he felt, give him enormous satisfaction.

Johnny was at that moment well out of his reach. With his pal, Peter, he was busy camouflaging the Invacar with sticks and bracken from the moor. Soon, hidden among some bushes, it was completely invisible. They took themselves to one of Johnny's regular hide-outs, a small cave at the side of a quarry, convenient as a bolthole and store. The stolen goods which he had collected were strewn about, things filched from shop counters – power drills, transistors, anything that could be flogged in the right quarter. Johnny's larder consisted of jars and packets of sweets. He handed some to Peter as they relaxed on two air-mattresses Johnny had stolen from a camping shop.

Peter admired Johnny. He couldn't keep up with him in enterprise, but had a boundless curiosity about his hero's way of life. Gazing round the fascinating cave, he asked, 'You living here, then?'

'No. Too bloody cold.'

'Where you living, then?'

'Old bloke's house – the one I donged the car off.'

'He lets you live there?'

'You're joking. Doesn't know, does he?'

Peter asked, through a boiled sweet, 'Why don't you live at home?'

'I bloody don't.'

'What's yer dad say when you're always running off?'

'He doesn't give a monkey's.'

'What about yer mum?'

'She's dead,' Johnny said shortly. He was not in the habit of talking about his mum.

'Are you sure?' Peter asked.

''Course I'm sure. Why?'

'Well, every time Dally Leonard's dad goes in the nick, they tell him his dad's very sick and has gone off to hospital in the country.'

'That's soft.' But Johnny was thinking about it. 'D'you think my mum could be ill in the country?'

'I don't know, do I?'

Johnny was letting himself think back. 'No, she's died. I'm sure of it. I remember her dying. There was the funeral, cakes and tea and sandwiches. I got three days off school. I remember that.'

'One day she'll come back,' Peter proffered. 'The Resicrution.'

Johnny sneered. 'I don't believe in religion. You can stuff it.'

'Do you remember your mum alive?'

'Aye.' The police had never seen the expression now on Johnny's face. 'She worked at hairdresser's. That was after Dad's accident. She always smelt of those beautiful hairsprays – lovely. Them smells was still in the house, still in the cupboards, after she was dead, you know . . .'

Peter was bored with the subject. 'Are you always going to run away from them?'

'Aye, until I'm grown up. Then I'm going to buy a cottage and settle down and get married.'

'Marriage is soft!'

'Only grown-ups have marriages,' Johnny reasoned. 'Kids never have them. You can bet anything that grown-ups have is fun.'

'What happens when the cops catch you?'

'They take me down the cells and put the boot in,' Johnny said importantly.

Peter sat up. 'Give you a kicking?'

'Bloody right.' But he was not convincing enough.

'I don't believe you.'

'*You* want a kicking?' Johnny invited, without stirring from his mattress. Such an invitation was understood to be purely academic, like the standard reply, 'Try it.'

'Where are you going to go in the car?' Peter inquired.

'Blackpool. Might, anyway. I daren't risk taking the main roads, the cops have got eyes in the back of their heads. They're not as dumb as they look.'

They were not enjoying the sweets by now, but they went on eating them.

Jean stood in the dormitory at St Edward's House, the council care home, beside the bed where Mr Macrae, the housemaster, said that Johnny slept when he was there. There were three other beds in the room, but no other occupants, Macrae told her. On a locker beside the bed were all Johnny's worldly possessions: a small pile of records, a grotesque stretch monster toy, in a poor state. The records had lost their sleeves. Jean picked up the top one. It was *Staying Alive*. Beside them lay two or three coloured biro pens and some stones formed in curious shapes. On top of the ordinary pillows was a smaller one, well worn and soiled, heart-shaped, with *Love One Another* written across it. Jean picked it up. 'What's this?'

'Oh, that's his cuddly pillow. He can't sleep at night without it. He usually takes it when he runs away – he'll sneak back for it.'

'In broad daylight? After stealing a car twice?'

'You'll see, he'll be back.'

Jean detailed Bentley to post himself on guard that night in the dormitory and wait. She didn't enjoy giving the order any more than Bentley would enjoy carrying it out.

It worked. As Bentley sat in the dark, the window deliberately left open was raised from outside, and a small figure stepped into the room. He had just reached his bed when Bentley pounced.

'Got you!'

Johnny fought like a tiger, dragging the constable to the ground with him and shrieking, 'You nasty bastard! Gimme it! Give me me cuddly pillow!'

Bentley let him take the pillow, while retaining a firm hold on him. Johnny buried his face in it and began to cry. Bentley wished he were on some other assignment, but at least he had carried out his Inspector's order.

chapter eight

It was Tom, in his Social Services capacity, who came up with a possible solution to the problem of Johnny Duffield. At the District Office he had heard of a similar case, though the lad had been older and moving towards serious crime. He had been adopted by a couple called Naylor. Tom, without consulting Jean, had telephoned Naylor to ask whether he would consider taking on another problem boy, and Naylor had said he'd like to meet Johnny.

Jean was dubious. She was beginning to give up hope that anything would mend Johnny's ways. The other boy had been an orphan, it appeared, which Johnny was not. Duffield Senior's permission would have to be got before anything could be done.

'You'd need a lot more than that,' Tom said, 'many other submissions and permissions. About a mile and a half of red tape, I'd say – adoption's one of the most difficult things to process. But shall we try it?'

'All right. Anything at all that *might* work . . .'

She liked the Naylors on sight when they arrived at the station. Mr Naylor was large, straightforward and, as Tom had said, ordinary. Mrs Naylor matched him – a pleasant-faced plumpish woman who looked capable of being kindly but standing no nonsense.

'Have a look at him,' she said to them. 'He was brought in last night and he's been very quiet all morning – tired out, I expect.'

'In the cells, is he?' Naylor asked.

'It's the only place where we can be sure of keeping him.'

They looked in through the square peephole of the cell door. Johnny lay asleep on the bunk bed, his face buried in his cuddly pillow. After a moment, Naylor asked his wife, 'Well? What d'you think?'

'He's not very big, is he? Not like Ronnie.'

'Don't judge him by size!' Jean warned her. 'You'll have to talk to him to get any idea of what he's like.'

The Naylors exchanged looks, and the husband nodded. 'All right.'

Johnny stirred and woke as the cell door was unlocked. He stared at them uncomprehendingly – two strange people, not the usual cops. He was more frightened than if a battery of policemen had entered. Jean spoke to him formally.

'John Duffield, I want to introduce you to Mr and Mrs Naylor. They'd like to talk to you.'

Johnny looked back at her blankly. When Naylor asked his age, he turned the same look on him.

'How long does he have to stay here?' Naylor asked.

'That's up to him. He's got to tell us where he's hidden an invalid car,' Jean said.

'And won't he?'

'No.'

'He's not a talker, that's plain,' Naylor said. For some reason this roused Johnny to speech.

'Go away and leave me me peace,' he muttered.

Naylor turned to Jean. 'I wonder if I could have a little chat with him alone? Just me and the lad.'

'Of course, we'll be outside.' She left the cell with Mrs Naylor.

Johnny was even more frightened, alone with Naylor. He stared back sullenly when Naylor offered him a bar of chocolate, retorting with his usual rudeness, 'Stuff it.'

'You're right,' Naylor replied amiably. 'Bad for your teeth. I'll eat it myself.' He peeled off the wrapping and sat contentedly eating, his eyes fixed on Johnny. As he had intended, the steady stare broke down the boy's defence of silence.

'What d'you want? Who are you?' he burst out. 'Bloody social worker?'

'No,' Naylor showed no signs of being offended. 'No, I'm not a bloody social worker.'

'Well, then, what are you? I don't have to sit here and listen to you, you know.'

As this was patently untrue, Naylor took his time. His

manner was slow, deliberate, calculated to calm the listener, even one as aggressively insolent as Johnny.

'I sell secondhand cars, in Balledge Road,' he said. 'By the way, where did you learn to tap the ignition on an Invacar?'

'I'm not answering any cop questions,' the boy snapped.

'I'm not asking them.' Naylor finished the bar. 'I understand your dad's a cripple?'

'No, he's a ballet dancer.'

Naylor nodded slowly as though he'd just received an expected and satisfactory answer. 'You're lucky to have a dad. I was an orphan, you know. Brought up in an orphanage in Darwen. They didn't soft-soap you in those days, and there weren't social workers – or bloody social workers, as you call 'em. In those days kids were really tough. They had to be, to survive.'

'*This Is Your Life*, then, is it? Where's Eamonn Andrews?'

Naylor appeared not to have heard. 'We've no children of our own, me and the missus. We've got a fostered lad called Ronnie – fourteen now – living with us. He's an orphan. He's been in trouble with the police – real trouble, I mean, not nicking invalid cars from old men who haven't got any legs to chase you . . . D'you like cars?'

Johnny showed a flicker of interest. 'Why're you asking?'

'I sell 'em. I've got thirty of 'em at the moment. There's a yard at the back of my premises which is private. Did you know it's legal for kids to drive cars around on private grounds? Ronnie, that's our fourteen-year-old, he's got an old banger I gave him. He drives it up and down t'yard all day.' He let a pause elapse, watching Johnny. 'Would you like to come and drive some of my cars?'

For once, Johnny didn't know quite what to retort. He assumed his gangster personality. 'I think I'm going to prison for a very long time.'

'I don't think you're going to prison at all, as long as you haven't banged up the Invacar or sold it.'

The dangerous gangster replied, 'You think I'll get off this rap? They won't let me see a lawyer, you know.'

'I think you'll get off the rap,' Naylor said with a smile. 'Are you going to tell 'em where you put the Invacar?'

'I don't know.' Johnny would have hated to admit it, but he was beginning to take to this man who was prepared to play his game. 'I'm thinking about it. It's the one card I've got left to play.' That was what they always said in films.

Naylor came out with his own trump card. 'Well, are you going to come and visit us and meet Ronnie, and drive some of my cars? Well? Yes or no?'

He was relieved to hear the boy say, 'Yes. Maybe . . .'

He rose, saying casually, 'My name's Jim. What's your Christian name?'

'Johnny.' A few minutes earlier he would have given a rude answer.

'All right, Johnny. See you soon.'

Jean was relieved and surprised to hear how the interview had gone, though it was far too early to be hopeful. She promised Naylor that she would make an appointment for him to meet Johnny's father.

Now that the boy was showing signs of cooperation, it seemed likely that he would agree to take them to the invalid car. With Johnny wedged firmly between herself and Beck they drove out to the moors, to the spot where he told them the car was hidden. A sharp wind was blowing over the moor; Bentley sneezed as they disembarked. They walked briskly, Johnny leading, without seeing anything that looked as though it might have given cover to a vehicle. Beck was getting suspicious. He swung Johnny round. 'Now, where is it?'

'I told you it's here.'

Jean surveyed the prospect, a fairly level stretch of moorland, the quarries some way off, a few melancholy-looking sheep. She, too, was beginning to have suspicions. 'I don't see it,' she said.

'Down there.' Johnny pointed to a hollow where a few bushes were clumped together. 'Behind those bushes.'

'I still don't see any car, and I don't believe those bushes are hiding one.'

As she spoke, Johnny was up and away, doubling back behind them, across the road and over a wall, out of sight.

'Get him! Get him!' Jean shouted. With the others she set

off in pursuit over the uneven ground which Johnny had skimmed over like a bird. They would have had about as much chance of catching a bird, in fact. They stopped, looking at each other in mutual reproach. It was almost incredible that he had got away yet again.

Jean was not best pleased on getting back to her office to find that Mr Cowley of the *Clarion* was waiting for her. He was in the Interview Room, poring excitedly over a map. It was, he said, the map of England; not an exciting piece of information to an Inspector with Johnny Duffield on her mind.

'Well, Mr Cowley?' she said as politely as possible.

'I'll tell you. I believe that this major arms cache, this possible headquarters of the Provisional IRA in England, is not a few steps from this very room. Between two motorways and on a straight line from Halifax.' He indicated a spot on the map. 'That's here, or hereabouts.'

'Look, I'm sorry. You've got hold of something the wrong way round, or something I know nothing about.'

'All I want from you,' he said earnestly, bringing the last lingering traces of the morning's Real Ale nearer to her, 'is the silent nod that I'm on the right track. From me – mum's the word. I'll say nowt about owt. But what I will have is some kind of story and background ready when the big announcement comes.'

'What big announcement?' Jean glanced at the clock.

Cowley said, with laborious patience, 'The announcement from the Anti-Terrorist Squad that they've found a headquarters, or a huge IRA cache round here.'

'Mr Cowley, I don't know what the hell you're talking about – I wish I did – and I can't help you.'

He rose majestically. 'You've made a decision which amounts fundamentally to a vote of no confidence in me. You'll find you regret it.' Map under arm, he departed, not hearing her call after him.

'I may have another story for you, later, about a boy.'

The interview between Jean, Naylor and Johnny's father went surprisingly well, Jean thought, after the chilly reception he had given her before. He received them in the early evening;

there was a bottle of stout beside him, and he had mellowed slightly over a glass or two. He listened attentively as Naylor talked to him of his own deprived childhood, and his wish to help children in the same sort of situation. He was told of Ronnie, the hard case, who had taken to life in the Naylor household and got himself sorted out, and of the car-driving which had helped him and given him an interest in life.

'It seems to me that what your Johnny needs is just that, an interest in life. He's got nothing to stay in one place for, so he runs.'

'Aye. That makes sense.'

Jean said, 'Would you give your permission for Johnny to go and stay with Mr Naylor for a trial period, Mr Duffield?'

'Yes. Okay.'

'Thanks,' said Naylor. 'Let's hope it'll work. Oh – there's a small problem in that the bobbies have gone and lost him again.'

'So I hear.'

'But no doubt in the fullness of time he'll surface. That's the hope, isn't it, miss?'

'More than a hope, Mr Naylor.'

The wind was getting up as they left the house, and there was a flurry of rain in it. It would be cold on the moor. Images of Johnny pursued her home. She hadn't meant to go on about him to Tom, but somehow it all came out as they ate the meal he had helped to cook. She saw that he was hearing, not listening. Carrying used dishes to the kitchen, she said, 'You're quiet.'

'Not really.'

'Sorry to keep bringing my work home. It's hard to switch off and not think about it.'

'That's fine, honestly. Don't think of it as work. I always want to hear all about it.'

'But you were thinking your own thoughts – what?'

'Well, you know – the usual list at the end of the day. My responsibilities. My inadequacy in dealing with them. I'm thinking, too, that we shouldn't have moved into this house.'

'Tom, we had to!'

'We didn't have to. There's no Home Office regulation that

you have to live in your section. We could have stayed in the old house.'

She ran hot water over the dishes in the sink, dried her hands, and faced him. 'What's wrong? Come on.'

Tom looked round the kitchen. 'I'm thinking it'll be a while before we get this kitchen finished, even if the units were cost-price. And it'll be a year before we can afford to carpet the upstairs. I'm thinking this job of mine is inevitably going to put us in a financial mess.'

She put a hand on his arm. 'You've too great a sense of responsibility, Tom. I don't know whether it's endearing or neurotic. Things like kitchens and carpets are unimportant, you know. I don't mind bare boards and half-completed kitchens. It's like when we were first married – not one possession in the world except the main one – each other.'

They were standing very close; he put his lips to her hair.

'Come on, you're going to get dewy-eyed and romantic, and we've got these dishes to do. Tell me more about the kid.'

'You know something? If I could have had children, if my various malfunctions hadn't counted kids out, the kind of kid I'd like to have had is Duffield. All the pros and cons of him, the backchat, the cheek, the impudence . . .'

Tom laughed. '"Con" is particularly applicable to the lad. So is "pro".'

'Isn't it just a bloody awful shame, though? There's a kid no one wants, and that's exactly the kid I'd have wanted. Don't worry, I'm not brooding. I've got you. And you're my over-generous gift from the gods.'

'Now you're getting romantic again.'

'No, just a little worried. You're to stop caring about the drop in wages with the new job. It doesn't matter. We'll manage the mortgage somehow. All I want is our happiness, and our happiness is you doing your job and me sorting out Johnny Duffield, and the two of us contributing something. Okay?'

'Okay,' he said. 'Don't worry any more about Duffield tonight.'

'No. But I wonder where he is . . .'

*

Old Mr Stainley was preparing his breakfast. He wheeled himself to and fro in his kitchenette, laying the tray as he laid it every morning. Then he brewed the tea, covered the pot with a cosy, and got down the biscuit tin that held his favourites. To his surprise it was empty. The day before there had been half a packet in it. Or he thought there had – could have been wrong, time played funny tricks sometimes.

Milk. He trundled to the fridge. In the milk rack stood an empty unrinsed bottle which had been full, not even started. Surely he couldn't have drunk it in an absentminded moment and put it back like that? Never. Now there'd be no milk for breakfast, if the milkman hadn't left any. He set off down the lobby towards the front door, and something else odd struck him. The door of the glory-hole, the cupboard under the stairs where he stored things, was open, and it was only ever opened when the cleaner came. He looked inside – and saw Johnny Duffield there, curled up on a pile of old mats and cushions, asleep.

Mr Stainley's loud cry woke Johnny, but before he could move the door was slammed on him and locked. As he kicked and yelled, Mr Stainley was summoning the police.

Two minutes before the Hillman Hunter containing Jean, Parrish and Beck arrived, Johnny's determined struggles had burst the slight lock, and freed him. He tore out of the house and down the street, pursued by the helpless old man in his wheelchair, just as the police car slowed down beside Stainley.

'The little bastard's on yon building site,' he told them, 'there, at bottom of street. Been sleeping in my house, nicking my milk and biscuits – it's him that took my Invacar . . .'

Jean said to Beck, 'I want this lad caught. I'll take no excuses this time. I want everybody, all of my men that's available, here, now . . .'

A squad car was on the scene within two minutes, four men in it.

The building site covered about two acres, rough cleared ground with a few ramshackle remains of buildings scattered on it, and a security fence hedging it in on three sides. Only one side offered a means of escape to the fugitive, Ranelagh Lane. Jean gave orders to have it sealed off. 'Right, now everybody stay put. Let's give it a few minutes and see if he breaks cove Beck relayed the order on his walkie-talkie.

'Naylor. Get the nick to phone Naylor,' Jean told him. 'Phone number's in desk entry, give him this location.'

A message came through from one of the constables. 'Joe, this is Maitland – I think I see the lad, back of that broken flue thing.'

'See him now?'

'No, just caught a glimpse. He's moving towards the exit to Ranelagh Lane.'

Beck warned the two constables nearing the exit to watch out. Two more squad cars arrived, with eight men in them. Jean deployed them to the possible escape area. Now, counting themselves, there should be enough to head the boy off if he made a run for it.

'Ma'am, I think we're covered. Shall we move in?'

'Right – but slow. I'll have the heads off the lot of you if Duffield gets away this time!'

The moving line of police was watched by a spectator who had just got out of his car. It was Mr Cowley of the *Clarion*. He marched angrily up to Jean.

'Thanks for your cooperation. I'll know how much value to set on your word in future, Inspector.'

'What *are* you on about, Mr Cowley?' she asked patiently.

'You're still denying this is the major arms cache of the headquarters of English IRA?'

'Oh, Mr Cowley, give over – please!'

A sudden cry from Beck. 'There he is!'

Johnny came out from the shelter of some huts like a rabbit bolting from a hole with a ferret behind it. He stopped, as he saw the numbers ranked against him, hesitated, then darted for a ruined building. But two large constables were there waiting for him. To and fro he ran, weaving and darting, too swift to be caught but unable to break through. Beck tried to grapple with him, lost him, and fell. Bentley took over, got a hold on the slippery creature and brought him to the ground, but was too slow to stop him scrambling up and dashing off again, round a corner and straight into Jean's arms.

Beck came up to help her hold on to him.

'Are you going to come quietly?' she asked Johnny. He was panting and seemed exhausted, but there was no telling with him.

'Aye,' he gasped.

'Are you sure?' Beck's voice was plaintive. 'Please, please don't run off again!'

Naylor had joined them and was listening.

Beck asked the boy, 'Are you going to show us where the stolen car is?'

'Aye, it's in Tanner's Quarry.'

'Can we take you there and you won't run off?' Jean asked.

'Aye, miss. I'm right out of breath, I won't run off again.'

'Thank you, Duffield,' she said warmly. 'Thank you very much.'

Naylor said, 'Now you've got him, can I have a word with him? I'll drive him to the quarry if you like.'

'Right, we'll follow you.'

Johnny sat very quietly in the car at Naylor's side. Naylor asked him, 'What d'you think they're going to do to you after this investment of police time, money and manpower?'

'I don't know,' answered the small voice.

'Well, I wish you a lot of luck, son.'

Johnny seemed to be thinking hard before he said, 'Well, after I've sorted this lot out, I'd really like to come round and drive your cars.'

'Ah. The problem is, are they going to let you? I don't think they will if you're always running away all the time and living on the streets and moors, like a stray cat.'

'Well, I think my living rough days are over, really.' Nobody had ever heard Johnny Duffield say such a thing before, or use such a grown-up tone. Naylor was delighted, but knew he mustn't show it too much.

'Well,' he said as they turned on to the moor road, 'I don't know what they're going to do with you, but if and when they get through with you, tell 'em to give me a ring and I'll come and collect you. Okay?'

Johnny looked up at him. 'Okay.'

*

On the building site, Mr Cowley strode up to the police car and knocked on the window to Jean.

'What's this, then – a load of hulking great bobbies chasing a tiny lad?'

'That's no tiny lad, Mr Cowley,' she replied sweetly. 'We have reason to believe that he's the Commander-in-Chief of the English Headquarters of the Provisional IRA.'

Cowley's face was the personification of disgust. 'Oh, very funny,' he said. 'Very, very funny indeed . . .'

chapter nine

'Yes, Mrs Melchett,' Jean said patiently. 'I do understand what you mean. But we talked about it before, and you agreed that you'd give it more time.' She was not over-pleased that Melchett's wife had called in instead of making use of Jean's personal office telephone number. It had been given to all the wives of her forty-three men, because wives often meant trouble. They got agitated about the danger their men ran into, about the irregular hours which led to wasted meals and frayed tempers, about the no-life a copper's wife often led. They saw safer jobs with better pay advertised, and nagged their husbands, sometimes to the point of resignation.

Jean didn't want it to come to that with Melchett. He was young, a little younger than her, keen and tough and Hartley born and bred. What there was to know about the local villains he knew, having grown up alongside them. He was invaluable. And she knew that he felt warmer towards her than did Beck, for instance. It was unfortunate that he was still newly married enough to listen to what his young wife said.

Mary Melchett was pretty, with a dark waterfall of hair and the face and figure of a fashion model, though lacking a model's inches. She had a sharp no-nonsense manner and a voice that would become shrewish with time. Jean felt herself being eyed, tested for vulnerability. Mary wanted a woman-to-woman combat for her man.

'I know I said I'd give it more time,' she said. 'That was before last Saturday. A quarter to midnight, it was, when he came in, with a big bruise on his face. I was half out of my mind, I can tell you, waiting for him. What sort of a life is that?'

'It's not a life, it's an incident. Something that happens now and then. Not all that often, in our part of the world. There'd been a demo in the afternoon that got violent. A lot of people got hurt and had to be taken to hospital. We took more statements that night than we've ever done here, Sergeant Parrish told me. That was why your husband was home late, Mrs Melchett. It may not happen again for a long time.'

Mary's full lips were mutinously set. 'That's all very well. But who's to say when it *will* happen again?'

'I can't tell you that, of course. You'll have to take a chance on it.'

'And what sort of chances is *he* taking? He could be killed, get a bang on the head that'd turn him into a cabbage. What about that?'

Jean shrugged. 'It's a risk he understands, and accepts.'

'Well, I don't. Do you know how old he is? Thirty-three. He could be doing a safe job for twice the pay. If he waits, he'll be too old.'

Jean drew a deep breath. 'Are you saying that your husband wants out?'

For the first time there was a hesitation. 'He's not said so. But he knows what I feel.'

'We've talked about this before,' Jean said, and God knew they had. As soon as possible after her appointment she had contacted the wives, and even young Davies's and Bentley's mothers, got them together and put herself at their disposal, preferably by telephone, so that she could talk to them when things went wrong. 'I said then that things could only get better in the Force. I told you that your husband had a lot of potential, that he could go a long way. That's still the case.'

'All right saying that, but . . .' The telephone rang. Into it Jean said, 'Yes, of course. Can you hold on? I've got someone with me.'

It was a formula that usually got rid of callers. Mary Melchett hooked her bag on her shoulder and got up swiftly. 'I'll come another time.'

'Will you have a good think first? What I've said makes sense, you know.'

When the door had shut she picked up the telephone again. 'Sorry about that. No, you didn't interrupt, love. Just somebody trying their strength. What's the trouble?' It was understood that Tom was free to telephone her from his office when problems arose that involved both their worlds.

He said, 'You don't want a cleaner, by any chance?'

'Not by any chance. I've got four good ones and they look like staying. Nobody pregnant, workshy or at death's door. Why?'

'We've got a case here, a young woman . . . I just wondered if anything could be done?'

The door opened to admit Detective Chief Inspector Wigan, with battle written all over his face. Jean waved him to a chair and said into the telephone, 'Can we talk about it later? Right. See you.'

Their supper was over before she encouraged Tom to talk about it, this newest case to crease his forehead and add to the abstracted air he so often wore now. Bit by bit he would be eaten up by his job, unless she managed to put some sort of check on him.

'Well?' she asked. 'What is it this time, this problem young woman?'

Tom lit his pipe. 'If you really want to hear about it . . .'

'I really do, and in any case I'm sure you're going to tell me.'

'All right. She's a Mrs Royle, twenty-eightish, two kids, husband gone down for five years. Armed robbery, GBH, watchman nearly done for. Dangerous type, Royle. He's been away two years now. She's got nothing but Social Security, and she says she can't manage, but it seems they won't give her a penny more.'

'Why?'

'No idea. Possibly they just can't give her any more because she's not entitled to it. She came to see us and we can't do anything, either. She's got a roof over her head – well, a flat of sorts – the kids are clean and decent-looking, but she worries about them a lot, says she can't manage. The Prisoners' Aid people have helped a bit, but it's still not enough.'

'Nothing ever is, for some people. She got the wrong side of somebody? Pushy manner, rough tongue?'

Tom looked shocked. 'Not a bit of it. I'd say she was a very gentle sort of girl.'

'Too pretty to please the ladies – other ladies?'

He hesitated. 'Very nice-looking. Appealing. But not what you'd call a bobbydazzler, no.'

Jean studied him. It had crossed her mind before that she might one day have to face the possibility of Tom's soft heart becoming entangled in the snares of another woman. She knew that she and he were so close that the woman would have to be a very remarkable one, but the possibility was there, as it always must be to a wife whose husband's work took him among all sorts and conditions. He was a handsome man, appealing to most women.

'Tom,' she said gently, 'don't get involved.'

He looked up, startled.

'I don't mean with Mrs Royle particularly. I've seen the way you look when you've been caught up with people's troubles. Did you ever do Keats's Letters at school? We did, in the last year, and though I wasn't exactly teacher's pet for Eng. Lit. I was really struck by those letters. He said that other people affected him very strongly – that their "identity" sort of attached itself to him. When he'd been to a party, he said, "not-myself comes home with myself". Or something. That's what I mean about you.'

'Yes.' Tom's face was grave. 'I do know what you mean. It's a danger anyone in social work has to face. All right, point taken.'

She sat back, relieved. 'And now go on about Mrs Royle.'

'With no involvement, then – the reason she can't take a job is the kids. The elder one's three, the other about eighteen months. She can't afford to pay a minder, and it'd be hard to find one who was all that willing . . . both the kids are difficult, she says. So the only job she could take would be one where they'd be with her.'

'And you thought – toddlers at the nick! Oh, darling, really! Can you see Beck changing a nappy?'

He joined in her laughter. 'No, of course, it was a ridiculous idea, just an impulsive thought. But seriously, do you think anyone there might know of a place where she could do cleaning, that sort of thing? All houses need keeping clean . . .'

'Such as this one?'

She had caught Tom completely by surprise. 'I didn't mean – I never thought . . .'

'I know you didn't, love. But it's a possibility. Just look round this room. All the attention it's had this week's been a lick and a promise. There's a film of dust on the mantelpiece because I haven't time to move the things off it. The paintwork wants a proper scrubbing. The whole house hasn't got over the move yet – and nor have I. I just can't do any more in the evenings, it's not on. So you see a vacancy exists, so to speak.'

'We can't afford it, Jean.'

'We might. For a bit, until we get absolutely straight. Let's keep the idea on file.'

Next morning, over breakfast, she said, 'I've been thinking about it some more, and I'd like to see this Mrs Royle of yours. I'll have to, before we even consider taking her on.'

Tom was torn in different directions. He had not imagined taking Mrs Royle into his own home, and he was not happy about the money a cleaner would cost. But he hated to see Jean doing household jobs until late at night, to keep the place up to her own high standard. Perhaps he'd been wrong to suggest anybody remotely connected with villains. After all, he met plenty of other people in the course of his work. He was glad that his programme for the rest of the week left him no time to approach Mrs Royle again.

That weekend, Jean's parents came on a visit. Their new Volvo was the big model, sleek and silver as a well-fed salmon, and Mrs Haywood was resplendent in a new coat of creamy lynx – fake, she was quick to point out, real fur being against her principles. Jean's father, a quiet grey man who cared now more for golf than anything else, nodded amicably from time to time as he was taken on a tour of the new house.

'Very nice, isn't it, dear?' Mrs Haywood inquired. 'Rather like the little place we started out in. Remember that funny scullery, and the people next door who did the washing every Saturday and hung it out just as people came to tea with us? I was really quite embarrassed. You'll have to get this kitchen finished soon, Jean, it's not adequate, is it? And you've got those horrid little things in the draining-board.'

'What horrid little things?'

'Silverfish. Ugh! There goes one now. They breed in damp wood, you know. Is that the same old fridge? Goodness, what a time you've had it. Aren't you due for a new one?'

'Do you know how much they cost? If it works, it stays.'

In the back garden, Jean's father said to Tom, 'You could have all this straight by spring.'

'If I'd the time . . .' He opened the door of a large shed. 'This is going to be my dark room. I had my eye on one of the bedrooms, but Jean's collared that for something else. It's nice and roomy in here, and there's a tap – couldn't be better. There was nowhere but some sort of antique washhouse at the other place.'

His father-in-law said, 'Jean's looking tired. Doing too much, is she?'

'She always does. It's a very demanding job. And she likes being what she calls fully stretched.'

Mr Haywood nodded. 'Aye, she always did. Pity it puts the years on, though.'

At teatime Blackie took it into his head to jump on Mrs Haywood's lap. Absently, chatting, she made him comfortable, then suddenly stopped stroking him.

'Jean! This cat's got fleas!' Dislodged, Blackie looked back reproachfully before settling down to wash.

'Has he? We hadn't noticed. Not surprising, I suppose, considering . . .' She decided not to reveal Blackie's life with Old Doris.

'You'll have to get rid of either him or the fleas, dear. They get into everything, simply everything. You'll need to Hoover the upholstery as well as the carpet, it's terrible how they spread. There's some stuff you can buy, but a real cleaning is what's wanted, a good carpet shampoo, and those covers going through the washing machine.' Mrs Haywood helped herself to a piece of the excellent cake Jean had bought that morning.

'Quite nice, this. You don't bake your own? I never think shop-bought's quite the same.'

'I haven't *time*, mother. I never shall have time, so we may as well all get used to this sort.'

That was when Tom made up his mind to introduce Jean to Mrs Royle.

The Royles' home was a small flat in a council block, on the second floor, approached by a flight of stone steps, which smelt faintly disagreeable but were reasonably clean to the eye. The front door, Jean noticed, was also clean; something that had been written on it in red chalk had been erased, though the mark still showed. Jean could guess roughly what the words had been.

Marilyn Royle looked startled and confused at the sight of Jean, as though what Tom had told her about his wife had not prepared her for the full effect of the uniform and Jean's air of authority. Or perhaps the sight of the uniform had brought a painful memory of her husband's conviction.

Tom introduced them, suddenly overcome by a feeling that he ought not to have brought Jean here. He saw her taking in the details of the flat – the narrow corridor, the living-room, a jazz-patterned carpet in fluorescent colours, floral wallpaper, a cheap modern sofa and armchair upholstered in patterned moquette, a table and four chairs in teak-style wood. A few photographs of children were dotted about the room; a toreador doll stood on the windowsill. It was all very predictable, but it was spotless and tidy. Jean got up and looked out of the window, which overlooked a car park.

She came straight to the conversational point. 'My husband tells me you've been having a bad time, Mrs Royle.'

The woman sat on one of the uncomfortable upright chairs, meeting Jean's eyes, though it was obvious that she was painfully shy. Somehow Jean had expected her to be small, perhaps because of the protective way Tom had talked about her. But she was only a little less tall than Jean herself, slender to the point of thinness, her face high-cheekboned and large-eyed, the mouth full and drooping in sad lines. A bell of hazel-brown hair fell softly round her face; it was not tinted or permed. A touch of the film star there, thought Jean, though certainly not the late Miss Monroe.

'Yes,' Mrs Royle said, and her voice was very soft, only just audible. 'Since Kevin went down. It's the two kiddies, you see.'

'Aged three and eighteen months, aren't they?'

The hair-bell nodded. 'The baby, that's Glenda, she can't walk yet. Slow, she is. But the Health people say she'll be all right.'

'And the other?'

'Trevor. He's a proper caution. Gets into everything.'

Oh dear, not a candidate for a private house. But Jean asked, 'Can I see them?'

Nodding again, Mrs Royle led her into the adjoining room, a bedroom. Jean's eyes took an instant snapshot of it, twin beds with Indian cotton bedspreads, a dressing table with a frilly skirt, everything very tidy, the 'Green Girl' picture on the wall behind the beds, directing her sultry glance into space. And, sitting on the floor occupied with a building toy, a small quick-eyed boy whom Jean guessed to be the image of his father. Behind him was a cot with a motionless bundle in it covered by a blanket appliquéd with pink rabbits.

''Ello,' said Trevor cheerfully. Then he took in Jean's uniform and his face lit up. 'You brought my dad back?'

'He saw him go,' Trevor's mother said in a shamed whisper. 'I didn't mean for that to happen, but he remembers.'

'No,' Jean answered, 'not yet, Trevor. What's that you've got? Can I see it?'

''S a cwane.' He demonstrated the crane, which he had put together very skilfully. Jean produced a loose button from her pocket and placed it on the crane's hook, which lifted and lowered it very satisfactorily. Tom watched from the doorway as Jean straightened herself and glanced into the cot. The pink sleeping face on the pillow was a type she had seen very often, and though it might well be as all right in time as the Health people said, she wouldn't have betted much on that. She noticed that a bathroom adjoined the bedroom, and said, with a smile which cancelled out any offence, 'May I have a look?'

The small bathroom was tiled and fitted out in pink, and it was spotless; clean towels, a few plastic toys neatly ranged on the bathrack, no obvious potties. A bathroom was the ultimate test of a woman's housekeeping. She remarked to Mrs Royle that it was pretty, and returned with her to the sitting-room.

'I hear you could do with a job,' she said. 'You seem to like housework, from the look of your flat.'

A shy smile. 'I like looking after things.'

'Other people's things?'

The startled-deer eyes were raised to hers. 'I've not been able to work.'

'No, but if you could?'

'I'd like that. Polishing. Dusting. Only . . .'

'Only people don't want the children?'

'No,' Mrs Royle whispered, a sad nymph, rejection in all the beautiful drooping lines of her head and shoulders. God, she's attractive, Jean thought, her eyes on Tom. But there was only compassion in his face, it seemed.

'If you had a job with someone who'd accept them, what would Trevor be like? Would he rush around smashing the place up? He looks a strong little lad.'

'He's strong all right. But he does as I say. He's never smashed a thing of mine, and he wouldn't anyone else's,' said Trevor's mother with a flash of spirit. Jean exchanged a long look with Tom, a question and answer in it on both sides.

'Mrs Royle,' she said, 'we need someone to clean our house. Not for always, perhaps – just until we get really straight after the removal. I could pay you the usual rates, and there's a bus stop just round the corner from us, if you could manage the baby on a bus. I'd pay your fare, of course. Twice or three times a week. Would that help?'

The girl's face came alive, trembling on the edge of smiles and tears, almost luminous in its beauty. 'Oh, missis, you wouldn't, would you? Give me a chance? It'd help that much, I can't tell you. Do you mean it? Mr Darblay did say something . . . but I didn't know it was for you.'

'I mean it. Of course, it would have to be for a trial period, on both sides. Okay?'

'Okay.' Marilyn Royle was smiling; it changed her completely. 'And I wouldn't let Trev be a nuisance, honestly. I'll bring his toys and he'll be as happy as anything, playing.'

'Good. It's not that we've a house full of priceless antiques, but what we have got we don't want to lose.' Jean mentioned terms, arranged days and hours, and they left. Marilyn Royle stood in the doorway watching them down the steps, the beatific smile still on her face.

'Lady Madonna,' Jean said when they were out of earshot.

'What?'

'Beatles number. About a girl with kids round her feet, making do somehow. Your Mrs Royle reminds me of that – only she's not a slut. You were right about her, love.'

'I hope I was. When I was there with Jennie Randall I thought the place looked very decent, but I knew you'd pick up anything that was wrong with it – or about her. It was a bit of a gamble.'

'Well, it paid off. She even manages to look well dressed, though she obviously doesn't get enough to eat. That was quite a classy shirt she had on. Anyone who looks after herself will look after our place, I hope . . .' Jean's eyes were on the road as she negotiated traffic, but a picture of the room they had just left was in her mind.

'No photographs of husband. What do you suppose that means? Either that she doesn't need reminding, or doesn't want reminding?'

'Who knows? Doesn't want would be my guess, from the information we've got on the files about him,' Tom said. He was glad that Jean had approved of his damsel in distress. But at the back of his mind an uneasy feeling lurked – the feeling that he might have brought something less than good into their home, and the fear that when he told his Senior Officer what he had done she might not be pleased. Ah, well. You had to take chances sometimes.

chapter ten

After a fortnight of Mrs Royle's domestic help Jean felt entirely happy about the arrangement. She had contrived to be at home for an hour one day in the first week, and had liked what she saw. Though the weather was cold, Trevor was firmly kept outside in the garden, adequately dressed in an anorak and warm trousers, the baby parked in her pushchair with a hood and rainproof cover over it. In the house Mrs Royle worked quietly, with thoroughness, as though she would be likely to overstay her arranged hours rather than skimp anything. She was methodical, careful-handed, washing china and glass as if it were her own. Jean noticed that she had brought rubber gloves to protect her hands; noticed, too, that at close quarters she gave off a faint fragrance which was unmistakably French and unmistakably good. It made a pleasant change from the stale fag-smoke which had hung around the place while workmen were in.

'Getting on all right, Mrs Royle?' she asked on her way out.

'Okay, thanks.' She was fastidiously dusting a small porcelain figure, a delicately coloured little lady in flowing skirt and poke bonnet. 'Pretty,' she said.

'You like our things?'

A nod.

'I noticed your scent – Dior, isn't it?'

'That's right. I've had it ages – took good care of it. Well, you've got to.'

'True. Now you know the routine – anything you need, replacements for cleaning stuff, you leave a note on the kitchen table and I'll see to it. Milk's in the fridge, I think there's plenty for the children. Oh, and a plumber might be calling to look at that pipe in the bathroom – he's from Barratt's.'

'Right.' Mrs Royle fought shy of any form of address. Jean

thought with amusement that the uniform probably confused her thoroughly.

Gradually the house began to lose the chaotic look it had worn ever since the removal, and even the bareness that came from the furniture from a small house being moved to a large one. Even the old yellowed paint looked better when it was clean. One day a note appeared, written in a large schoolgirlish hand:

I am not bad at painting if you would like some done if I could have a extra hour.

'Fantastic,' Tom said. 'I've been meaning to do it ever since we moved, but I can't see that I'll ever get the time. Tell her I'll buy the paint and leave it for her.'

'I hope she won't make a mess, that's all. The place looks better shabby than it would with paint slopped all over. And Trevor's sure to want to get involved. Are you sure?'

But Mrs Royle's painting was as neatly and professionally done as her housework. What had been dingy before was now sparkling white. Another note appeared:

Thanks for the extra money I would not mind staining the bedroom floors walnut would look nice.

Jean said, 'Well, if she wants to . . . It's a nasty job, crawling around on all fours. Won't it spoil her hands?'

'I expect she needs all the money she can get. Our budget's slipping, love. We can't afford someone as versatile as Mrs Royle!'

'In for a penny . . . She enjoys it, we appreciate it, and once it's done it's done. If it turns out well we might even do some entertaining.'

It turned out well. Jean looked through her diary and found an evening that looked quite clear, barring accidents. 'Right,' she said. 'We'll have the Wigans to dinner. Time we had someone, and we might as well start with them.'

'Is that a good idea?' Tom asked. He knew the ambivalent situation between Chief Inspector Wigan and Jean, his inferior in rank but his equal when it came to arrangements within her own domain, the Section. The atmosphere had been very strained during her first weeks at Hartley, as Wigan fought against her exercise of authority and showed clearly his resentment at having to accept it. Women in charge were not in his book. His pride was sensitive and his temper had a low flashpoint.

'Yes, it is, a very good idea. I've been working hard on Jack. It can't do any harm to give him a good dinner and let him talk about himself without being interrupted. Not much point in being a woman if one can't use it.'

Wigan accepted the invitation, on behalf of himself and his wife, stiffly but with a gleam of gratification, Jean noticed. Not a popular man, he was unused to entertainment that was neither official nor civic. He should have, she decided, the sort of meal that was as different as it could be from the usual public dinner menu of synthetic prawn cocktail or melon, chicken with frozen vegetables and sweet liberally dolloped with something that looked and tasted like shaving-cream.

What she would present him with was a first course of smoked salmon from the supermarket fridge – expensive but delicious, with brown bread and butter and lemon slices – followed by her own version of Boeuf Bourguignonne, prepared the night before after the beef had sat for twelve hours in a marinade of red wine. They were lashing out on wine, something they didn't let themselves indulge in except for special occasions; Tom had found some ends-of-bins at a wineshop which bore good names and belonged to good years. For a sweet there would be a simple fruit salad, made from whatever fruits were available. She was a plain cook, nothing elaborate, but what she served would be good.

The Wigans were early. Jean met them in the hall, calm and smiling, showing no trace of the spin she had been in since getting home after a last-minute delay at the station. She wore a long dress of Indian cotton from one of the Pakistani shops, orange-gold with touches of scarlet, dangling gilt filigree earrings from the accessories counter, and a false hairpiece whose dynel curls exactly matched her own hair and, pinned on at the back, gave the impression of graceful long locks. She looked quite another woman from the one Wigan was used to seeing. He registered surprise and, though he was not used to showing it, admiration. So long as he doesn't pigeon-hole me as a Little Woman who should stick to hearth and home, she thought. But there was not much danger of that, Jack Wigan being what he was.

Mrs Wigan was small and dumpy. She smiled a great deal, looked older than her husband, and agreed with or echoed everything he said. In Jean's experience didactic men had either wives who drove them into it by bossiness, or the other kind who let them have their own way at home, so that they expected to get it everywhere else.

As she ushered them into the dining-room, discreetly underlit so that the absence of much furniture wouldn't be noticed; congratulatory remarks flowed, mainly from Mrs Wigan. 'What a pleasant house – how individual you've made it – so nice to see a real fire on a cold night, really cosy.' Jean was pleased by the effect of the silver cutlery on the table, part of the canteen of plate her mother had given them for a wedding present, by the tablemats with their scenes of Pennine country, and the four good wine glasses of Stuart crystal – all they possessed. Mrs Royle had polished what furniture there was to shining point with some preparation which left a lavender fragrance behind.

'Goodness,' Mrs Wigan said, 'how hard you must work to keep everything like this! And Jack tells me you've not been here long. How ever do you do it?'

'Well – we have a Treasure. Quite young, but one of the old-fashioned kind as far as work goes.'

'How lovely for you – aren't you lucky! We lost our old dear, didn't we, Jack, twenty-four years she'd been with us. Arthritis, you know, Mrs Darblay.'

'Jean, please.'

'Jean, then. And I'm Mabel.'

From then onwards everything went perfectly. Tom, emerging from last-minute supervising in the kitchen, went down very well with Mrs Wigan and behaved to her husband with his usual quiet tact, letting the Detective Inspector do as much talking as he liked. Over the sherry he unwound; over the wine with which Tom generously topped up his glass he became positively genial.

'Beautiful, this, Jean,' he said of the beef. 'Why didn't you tell us you could cook?'

'It didn't arise. I'm glad you like it. More?'

'Thanks. Better than that stuff they do at the pub. You know what they say? That there's a shortage of cats in Hartley, since the locals started doing hot food.'

'Jack!' his wife protested with a giggle.

'Well, I don't know, but that's what they say.' It occurred to Jean that the watery bitter all the lads drank at the pub was his staple drink, and that the reasonably good wine which Tom had got to just the right temperature was going to his head. At this rate he wouldn't be able to drive home. She wondered if Mrs Wigan, who was more abstemious, could take over ...

The fruit salad was brought in, cool and refreshing after the strong tastes of the first two courses. Jean eyed with satisfaction the growing piles of crockery on the draining board. Not for her and Tom the dreary midnight donning of pinafores to get the stuff washed up. Mrs Royle had promised, in one of her laconic notes, to come and do it all in the morning. Another £3 of extra time, but just for once it was worth it. She devoted herself to being charming and talking well, as she could talk. She knew that Wigan would never regard her in quite such an unfavourable light again; the situation would not have changed, but she had put him under a subtle obligation. If it were only possible to have Beck to dinner ... but it wouldn't do, at all.

As they settled to the dessert the telephone rang. Tom apologized and went to answer it. Some instinct told Jean, before he came back, what it would be.

'There's been a multiple smash-up, corner of Union Street and Tilekiln Lane. At least two dead, and they haven't got at the occupants of one of the cars yet. I'm sorry, Jean, but you're wanted.'

There was no way round it; an emergency was an emergency. 'I'm very sorry, Jack and Mabel, but you know how it is. Will you forgive me? Tom will look after you. I haven't a hope of getting back for at least a couple of hours ...'

It was fortunate that they were the sort of guests who understood. Wigan had himself plenty of experience of emergency calls – it could happen in the middle of the night or on Christmas Day.

'It's all right,' Tom said to her, out of the room. 'I'll get the coffee and the liqueur.' They had invested in a bottle of cut-price brandy. 'Don't worry, they're enjoying themselves.'

'I've quite enjoyed *my*self in a sort of way.' She ran upstairs and changed rapidly. No question of going to an accident or a crime in evening dress – only her uniform brought her attention and respect, and even with it on she had to make it very plain that she was not merely a WPC. Off came the Indian gown, the earrings, the hairpiece. In five minutes she was the Inspector again, off to the scene at the wheel of her Mini. She was thankful that her routine carefulness about drink had kept her fit to drive; there was an art in holding on to the same glass of wine for a long time.

The accident was complicated and bloody. There were streets to be cordoned off, statements to be taken, a long cold vigil while two victims were cut out of their wrecked Cortina, and those who couldn't be helped taken away on covered stretchers. Davies and Bentley were there, shocked but calm about it. Jean went in the ambulance with the last people to be rescued, a young man and a girl, terribly injured. At Casualty she went through their belongings with Bentley, found names, addresses, a telephone number. The same was done for the five other victims, three of them dead, before the most unpopular police job of all had to be done, the informing of relatives.

It was four o'clock in the morning when Jean got home, Bentley driving her. She disliked being helped out of cars, but he put a solicitous hand lightly under her arm as she crawled out.

'All right, ma'am?'

'Yes, perfectly. Thanks, Roland. Go and get some sleep yourself. And say I'll be in a bit late tomorrow, will you?'

In fact she slept through the alarm she had set. Tom was gone from their bed, sunshine coming into the room. She leapt up, glad that habit had made her hang up her uniform and put trees in her shoes; after the quickest of showers she would be ready to leave again in a quarter of an hour or so.

In the kitchen there were sounds. She looked in, to see Mrs

Royle placidly dealing with the pile of crockery, cutlery, dishes and saucepans.

'You *are* early! How splendid. Is there anything you want to ask me today? Because I must dash.'

'Only I got you a bit of breakfast – Mr Darblay said you was to have it, so I put it on when I heard you upstairs.'

'Coffee and toast! Mrs Royle, you're a marvel. I shouldn't stop but I can't resist it.' She was extremely glad of the hot drink and the crisp toast. There'd be something at the station, but it made all the difference to set off from home with sustenance inside one. The gruesome scenes of the night receded. Through the kitchen window Trevor could be seen running round and round the lawn in what looked like a monotonous exercise but was doubtless some absorbing game. His baby sister, strapped into her shabby pushchair, watched him steadily, her expression slightly less vacant than usual. Blackie sat in the sun on the coalshed, washing. Life was back to normal. Thank God for Mrs Royle . . .

Jean was preparing the meal that evening when Mrs Fairweather gave her usual timid ring at the bell, as though a bird had flown into it and immediately fluttered away.

'Oh, Mrs Darblay, I *am* sorry to bother you . . . I just wanted to ask . . .'

Jean could hear sizzling from the grill. 'Come in a minute,' she said, hoping that the minute would be just about that. In the kitchen Mrs Fairweather commented on the good smell, the pleasant view, the general tidiness of things, which brought her to the point.

'I just wondered . . . that young woman who cleans for you. Such a nice-looking girl, and the kiddies don't seem at all a bother. I can't help noticing, you know, being only next door.'

'Yes, she's excellent.' Jean turned the cutlets, aware of a hungry Tom waiting for his supper.

'I'm sure it must be a relief for you, having her here, with your important job. It makes all the difference, doesn't it, a good Help. Mrs Roberts, at thirty-one you know, well, I don't care at all for her lady; belongs to those people that come to the door asking if you're saved. Sings hymns all the time, Mrs Roberts says. At least she's honest, that's something. Mrs Bagot at the end got one that *took things*, not that there was a lot to take . . . I'm sure your Mrs Whatshername is honest.'

'So far as I know, perfectly.' Jean ostentatiously banged plates into the warming rack and shook up the vegetables. Mrs Fairweather took the hint.

'It's all getting a bit too much for me, you know, not being very strong, and then my hubby with his back. So I thought . . . if you don't need your lady every day, could she give me a bit of time, do you think?'

Jean temporized. 'I'm not quite sure, without asking her. I don't think she has another place, but I'll find out and let you know.'

To Tom she said later, 'Do we really want her going next door? The old dear's a terrible fusspot, and if she rubbed our Marilyn up the wrong way she might get put off, and leave altogether. It's not that I mind sharing – well, yes, I do. I don't very much want gossip about this house going into that one, for another thing.'

'Would Mrs Royle gossip? She seems a very silent sort of girl.'

'I should think there might be a bit of fishing on Mrs F.'s part – domestic details about police private life, that sort of thing. I don't know. I'd have to warn her about that.'

'It'd be more money for her,' Tom said. 'She's looking better for being here, and a bit more might put her right outside the trouble-line.' It was true. Over the weeks Marilyn Royle had lost some of the stranded-mermaid look she had had the first time Jean saw her. Now she had a kind of bloom, it was possible to see how very attractive she was. The air of their district was probably much better than that of her own dingy street.

'I'll ask her tomorrow, if I decide it would be a good idea,' Jean said. 'No, I can't. I don't pay her till Saturday.'

'That reminds me. I've asked the insurance man to come up tomorrow. We can't leave it any longer, can we; I've been putting it off because I know the premium's going to be high, but this house is worth a lot more than it was, with the repairs we've done, and if it burnt down next week we'd be sorry. To put it mildly. Did you know that if the walls are left standing they don't consider you qualify for a new house, cost of?'

'Yes, I did, though a lot of arsonists don't. Do you want me to be here?'

'If you like. Yes, come up if you can. I arranged for one o'clock, so that I could have a bit of lunch at home.'

For once Jean's Thursday morning was quiet – a parade, a long report to read, Parrish dealing patiently at his desk with a nutter, letters to dictate. By 12.30 she felt free to go home for an hour or so. It was better that she should be there, knowing herself to be that much more practical than Tom in money matters and being, at the moment, the principal breadwinner.

Tom had just arrived; she parked her car in the road, leaving him the space in front of the garage.

'No insurance wallah yet?'

'Not yet. You're good and early, love. Shall we start our snack before he comes? I got some of that cheese you like from the delicatessen.'

'Right, wheel it in. I'll make some coffee.'

From the pantry Tom called to her. 'This window's open. Should it be?'

'No – there's a ventilator. It's never opened.'

'Well, it is now.'

She joined him. The narrow sash-window over the table that held tins of flour, a bread bin and sundries was pushed up about eighteen inches.

'Mrs Royle probably opened it to let some air in and forgot about it,' Tom said.

'It's the first time, then.' Jean surveyed the table. 'These things have been moved – there's some flour spilt on the floor.'

They looked at each other, the same thought in their minds.

'There's someone in the house, or there has been,' Jean said. 'Right, let's start looking.'

'Keep behind me.' Tom led the way into the sitting-room. There was a look of disorder in it and some empty spaces. One was where the little porcelain lady had been. The transistor radio was missing. Jean pointed to a blank on the wall below a picture-hanger. 'What was there?' Tom asked.

'A group photograph of the Training College. It was in a silver frame. And my award, the little silver cup, that's gone. And so has the carriage clock.'

'Well, he's not down here.' Tom had opened the serving-hatch and glanced into the dining-room.

'And I don't suppose some of the silver plate is, either.' Jean went in and began opening drawers. 'No – about half of it gone. Some villains have got taste. Come on, upstairs. Better take the poker in case he's still there showing fight. God, fancy this happening in your own home. I know now how it feels!'

At the top of the stairs Tom said quietly, 'Listen.' There were sounds in their bedroom, scuffling noises, then the distinctive sound of a window being pushed up. Tom flung the door open, pushing Jean behind him, ignoring her resistance.

The young man was cowering in the window bay, one leg over the sill, terror in every line of him. He was shortish and dark, his hair the length that Jean wouldn't allow on her young constables. He wore the uniform of his kind, bomber jacket and old jeans. As they moved forward he glanced desperately out of the window, calculating the distance.

'I shouldn't,' Jean said. 'There's a twenty-foot drop to a concrete path. Come on in and let's have a look at you.' She saw that he was literally shaking. On the floor between them were two pillowcases taken from the rumpled bed, bulging with objects. The wardrobe door was open, and so were most of the drawers in the dressing table and chest, garments spilling out of them. Jean's Indian dress lay in a bright heap on the floor and her best coat was flung over a chair.

'All right,' she said. 'What's your name?'

He tried, unsuccessfully, to speak, then got out, 'Terry Maxwell.'

'Address?'

'Rathbone Buildin's.'

'I see.' Jean did, all too clearly. 'And you broke in all by yourself?'

'That's right.'

'It isn't, you know. You were let in. Weren't you?' Tom was standing beside her, the poker in his hand in case the youth decided to attack, but that was the last thing he seemed likely to do. After a pause, he nodded. 'Aye, I were.'

'Got form, have you? I can guess, a few jobs; not a lot judging by the mess you've made of this. Come on, downstairs, I'm taking you in. Keep a grip on him, Tom, in case he gets slippery.' They went downstairs in procession, Terry Maxwell almost drooping between his two formidable captors. Tom pushed him into Jean's car. 'I'll come with you,' he said.

'No need – he won't give trouble, will you, Terry?' She spoke into her walkie-talkie to a startled Sergeant Parrish, then started the car, the boy sitting white and silent beside her.

In the Interview Room he appeared even more frightened, and Jean sensed that he would talk. Davies sat, pencil and pad at the ready for the information that came easily.

'I thought there'd be nobody in,' Terry said. 'She told me there wasn't ever, daytime.'

'"She"?'

'Marilyn. Marilyn Royle.'

'Yes. You live in the same flat-block, of course. What else did she tell you?'

'Said it would be easy. She'd leave the window open, and I could shut it after me and let meself out the back door. I'd got a van – round the corner. I've done a few jobs before, like you said. I were one of Kevin's mates before he went down, you know.'

Yes, I know, thought Jean. A daft young lad tagging round after an older man, a villain with a record and a great reputation; a layabout who'd like to be the same sort of tearaway as his hero, only he hadn't the guts. A lad who'd hung round his hero's lonely wife afterwards.

'Expecting a good haul from my house, were you?' she asked.

'She said you'd got some nice things . . . That's what I done it for, to give 'em to her. I were going to sell a few, but mostly they was for her.' He was losing some of his fright in the effort to explain himself, possibly save himself punishment. 'She liked nice things, see, things like you had, missis, only she wouldn't nick 'em herself, she's too straight, so I said I'd do it, then you'd never know she'd owt to do with it.'

Davies was writing busily.

'Had you nicked things for her before?' Jean asked.

Terry nodded. 'When I were working – I were on strength at Blackett & Hurst's for a bit. We'd be doing plumbing repairs, or kitchen jobs – I'd go to the upstairs lav and nip into the bedroom, same time. Scent, and that. She likes scent. That were how—'

'How you got fired. Right, I think we've got enough. Detective Constable Davies will give you your statement to sign.' She got up, Terry's gaze following her nervously.

'What'll they do with me?'

'How do I know? You've told us what happened, that should help, and we've got the loot back.' Something in his face made her add, '*Have* we? All of it?'

Not looking at her, he fished in an inside pocket and pushed something over the table towards her. Her Indian filigree earrings glittered up at her. She knew she could never wear them again.

'Can I have a ciggie now?' Terry asked.

'Feel free.' Jean turned on her heel and left the Interview Room.

When she got in that evening Tom asked her, 'How did it go?'

'Okay. No trouble, no complications.' Her voice was laconic; Tom guessed why.

'I haven't tidied up,' he said, 'in case you wanted fingerprints.'

'No, no dabs needed. Let's go and get it over before we eat.'

The pillowcases, emptied out, revealed the missing objects from downstairs, the little clock, the silver cup, the photograph and Queen's Plate cutlery, other small things they'd not missed before. Along with them were Tom's ivory-backed brushes and his electric razor, Jean's best lingerie, slips, tights, two filmy nightdresses, a bikini worn on her rare holidays, and the only bottle of expensive scent she owned.

'She told him exactly what to take and where to find it,' Jean said. 'She went through the drawers, time and time again, I daresay, making a note of the things she wanted. Probably gave him a list. Day after day, checking out my possessions.'

'How could she know they'd be any use to her – these clothes?'

'Because we're roughly the same size and height. I'm a bit taller and a bit squarer, that's all. Oh, she knew.'

Tom put his arm round her. 'It's a rotten feeling, isn't it? She seemed so . . . you were so good to her, and it was all working out so well.'

'What we didn't see was that she was stupid. Too stupid to realize that she was the first person we'd connect with the burglary. Stupid enough to think she could wear my clothes in this house, probably, and I wouldn't notice.' And not caring about my feelings at all, she thought, mechanically picking up scattered garments, folding them and putting them in a pile. Not grateful one bit, for the work I gave her that nobody else would. Not interested in what I'd feel about losing the best of my things. A policewoman's life isn't exactly packed with appreciation, but just now and then you come across someone who actually seems to like you. This had been one of those times.

Tom said, looking round, 'It's a loathsome feeling, that a stranger's been in your house, handling things, looking at what's personal to you. As though a snail had crawled over everything, leaving its trail.'

'That's what most of them say – the people who've been done. Some of them move house afterwards.' She looked down at the pile of garments. 'I'm going to wash this lot before I put them away again. And don't tell me they're clean.'

Tom had not been going to.

When they went out next morning they left the house locked, the back door Mrs Royle used bolted on the inside. Jean knew she would not be coming that day. When half an hour showed clear in her day's programme she went to Rathbone Buildings and rang firmly at the bell marked *Royle*.

Marilyn Royle was there, waiting. Her eyes slid past Jean for more uniforms.

'No, there's nobody else,' Jean told her. 'Just me.' She shut the door behind her, noticing that the baby had been strapped into its pushchair and Trevor was wearing his boots. So their mother had expected to have to leave.

'You know about it? Your boy friend getting caught in the act?'

A silent nod.

'He's still down the nick – we haven't finished with him yet.'

'He only done it for me. He knew Kev never gave me nice things, and I can't afford none. He done it out of good-heartedness.' There was no emotion in the girl's voice, only plain statement of fact.

'Didn't you realize you were lining yourself up with your husband, inciting someone to housebreaking so that you could receive the stolen goods?'

'No.'

'You're lucky not to be down there with your friend Terry. You will be, before long, if you go on like this. Then what will happen to these two kids? I'll tell you – they'll be taken into care. Glenda will probably be put into an institution for the mentally subnormal.'

It was a cruel thing to say, though meant only as a warning, but it drew no blood; the blue eyes looked steadily back at Jean. There was a chain round the girl's neck with a locket hanging from it, easily recognizable as antique. Just one of the things that had come from Terry's excursions into bedrooms. As though the remark about the baby had been a signal that the worst of the telling-off was over, Marilyn said, 'Is it all right, then?'

'Is what all right?'

'Me job. It won't make any difference, will it?'

Jean had remained standing. Now she sat down. 'Mrs Royle,' she said, 'do you think I could ever trust you again? I couldn't employ you, knowing what you're capable of. I couldn't recommend you to anyone, either. You must see that. I've got a neighbour who'll put the story round as it is.'

Marilyn suddenly broke. Tears poured down her cheeks, she collapsed in a chair, great noisy sobs came from her. Trevor, half-way through a chocolate bar, began to roar too, burying his face against her leg.

'You won't take me job away, missis?' she gulped out. 'I've nowt else, only the bit of money they give me. Oh, don't take me job, please don't! I can't manage . . .' Her beauty was gone, obliterated with the distortion of weeping. Jean pitied her very much, but pity was not the answer.

'Marilyn,' she said gently, 'it's not my choice. There's nothing more I can do for you. Thank you for all you've done for me. You're a great worker.' She got up. 'I'll ask my husband to talk to Social Security about you.'

Half-way down the stone stairs the sound of the harsh weeping was still coming from the flat.

Tom listened gravely when she told him. 'You couldn't have done anything else. I'm only sorry I got you into this in the first place. I ought to have known better. One gets carried away when one's a novice at the job.'

'All right. I won't say I told you so, because I didn't. I was taken in, too. But there was something I did tell you – don't get involved.'

'I know, and you were dead right. I won't, in future.'

I only hope you mean it, love, Jean thought.

chapter eleven

The departure of Mrs Royle from the household had a depressing effect on Jean. It would be perfectly possible to find another domestic help in a town with a high unemployment rate, but the interviewing of candidates and checking up their characters all took time she could little afford. Meanwhile, she found herself back at square one – doing the housework and cooking herself, giving to these things the time that should have been hers and Tom's. Their life was beginning to suffer, she knew, and there was little she could do about it.

Tom was getting too many of his own meals, for one thing. He had always been prepared to do this, and to put up with the inevitable semi-instant meals Jean provided – omelettes, chops, frozen fish, things that were little trouble to prepare and cooked quickly. His patience and tolerance were great, but he was only human, and sometimes couldn't help a slight weariness showing. He accepted, had always accepted, that he had a career woman for a wife, and that was fine, except when he would have liked her to be just a wife. She was objective enough to be able to feel her official personality lingering over into her private life, just as Tom's now did, though he didn't realize it. As a design engineer he hadn't brought his work home; now he did, and Jean was unhappy about its effect on him. She knew that he was vulnerable to the wrongs and distresses of others; more vulnerable, perhaps, than a social worker should be. In her own job she had learned toughness and detachment in dealing with the same sort of problem cases as those Tom handled. She hoped very much that their lines would never cross and bring them into conflict with each other over an issue.

Which was what happened in the case of the Murphy family.

It began the morning that Sergeant Parrish greeted her with the news that there was a drunk and disorderly in the cells.

'Stole the yellow balloon off a zebra crossing, hit Constable Farley on the shoulder with it, then smashed it against a wall. Picked up at four a.m.'

'Name?'

'John Michael Murphy.'

'Known?'

'Quite well. We've seen him in here, over the years.'

'Right, I'll have a look at him,' she said. 'Is Sergeant Beck on his way to Coleman Parade?'

'Yes, ma'am. Ought to be there by now.'

'I'd like a word with him.' Parrish handed her the radio microphone, and resumed his consumption of one of his favourite bacon rolls.

Passing Coleman Parade, a row of derelict old houses, on her way in, Jean's attention had been caught by something curious about one of the houses. They were eyeless, their windows and doors sealed off by sheets of corrugated iron against the entry of squatters or children. Yet from the chimney of number nineteen smoke was drifting. She radioed instructions to Beck to investigate.

He confirmed that he could see the smoke and was about to let himself into the house, by some means or other, sounding a trifle put out at having been sent on such a job. He had neither the build nor the athleticism to make harlequin leaps through windows, and his eventual entry through a window at the back of the house was neither graceful nor dignified, and drew from him strong language. The room he finally managed to wriggle into was empty. It had obviously been empty a long time. Dusting himself down, he went along a dark narrow passage to the front room.

It was completely dark, its window boarded up more firmly than the one by which Beck had entered, but for the thin flickering of a fire in the grate. It showed him a girl, huddled against a wall, still with terror. He shone a torch on her, taking in her thin arms and legs, her face which might have been pretty if it had not been disfigured by great bruises. She was about sixteen he reckoned. She was very afraid of him.

'So who are you, then?' he barked. 'What are you doing trespassing here?'

She said nothing, only shrank away, staring, big-eyed.

'Well? Are you going to tell me your name here, or down at the police station?'

At last she whispered, 'Maeve Murphy.' Her voice was as Irish as her name suggested.

'Address?'

'Thirty-nine Salford Road.'

Something clicked in Beck's memory. 'You wouldn't happen to be the daughter of John Murphy, at the moment in police custody?' No answer.

'Is John Murphy your dad?'

She nodded.

'I thought so.' He studied her. 'Now where did those bruises come from? All right, don't tell me. You'd better come along with me, young woman.'

'I can't walk proper,' she said. 'He kicked me ankle, and I think me other knee's twisted.' As she took a step forward she gave a cry of pain and staggered, as the ankle gave way under her. Beck caught her. It occurred to him that John Murphy was at that moment in the best place for him.

Jean had not yet got round to interviewing Murphy. She was talking to a new arrival in the Section, Sergeant Margaret Cullinane, in Hartley on a compassionate posting. She was twenty-five, slim, with the sort of figure which looks well in uniform; her bright sweet smile offset a crisp no-nonsense manner. Jean liked the look of her. Her documents said that she had been three and a half years in the Service. So she'd had a rapid promotion. Just off a special course, Hartley-born, home in Preston, married.

They surveyed each other across Jean's desk, Maggie Cullinane with her confident smile. Jean already knew the facts, but talking them over mattered.

'Compassionate posting,' she said. 'What's the problem?'

'My mother, ma'am. She has to undergo a hip replacement operation at Hartley General tomorrow. She's sixty-nine. I wasn't going to make a request for a compassionate posting. but my Chief insisted.'

'I see. And how long will you be here do you reckon?'

'If all goes well, a few days – if it doesn't, maybe a fortnight, maybe more. It's her second operation – the first one didn't take.'

Jean was making unnecessary notes. 'Sergeant Parrish will look after you – explain the ropes and which ones to pull, and which not to, and why and when.'

'Yes, ma'am.' Sergeant Cullinane's tone was correctly respectful, but she looked as if she knew all the possibilities already.

Jean said, 'To get things straight – could I ask you to observe two house rules here? One, I'm the only woman on strength in this station. I've noticed my particular bunch of males react quite poorly to any policewoman who comes by and starts throwing Women's Lib ideas around. Understood?'

The Sergeant understood.

'Two, we had a particular policewoman here before who criticized everything the previous shift got up to. Do you think you could avoid that – criticizing the activities of the previous shift?' There was no harm in dropping a hint to this sharp young woman, who answered, predictably. 'I'm not here to make any trouble, ma'am.'

Jean hoped that was true. She thought it might be. 'Are you ambitious?' she asked.

'Yes, ma'am.'

'What do you want out of the Service?'

This time the answer was not so predictable. 'I want your job.'

After a fractional pause, Jean asked, 'To be in charge of a Section?'

Sergeant Cullinane met her eyes fearlessly. 'I spent my childhood in Hartley. I want to be in charge of *this* Section, ma'am.'

'You're very blunt.' Jean couldn't help being amused or wondering, just a little, where this compassionate posting would end. 'I'm the incumbent here,' she added, 'and here I stay, for the foreseeable.'

'We can never tell what's going to happen with our futures in the Service, ma'am, can we?' was the slightly pert reply. Jean left it unanswered.

'See if you can find Constable Bentley, and tell him we're waiting for our coffee. I'm going down to the cells.'

John Michael Murphy had been raving, with himself as an audience, for some time before Jean and Parrish took a look at him through the peephole of his cell. He had no objection to doing without an audience for his wild ramblings, being quite happy to admire his own verbosity, which meant absolutely nothing and was derived from the ramblings of his predecessors, who had lived for many years on legends of the Troubles loosely based on Yeatsian phrases. Only, John Michael Murphy had never heard of Yeats, and had only seen the plough and the stars through the bottom of an upturned glass. He was middle-aged, roughcast, fanatic of eye; Jean took a dislike to him on sight, trusting her instincts to point out a man who raved about human rights and emotions from a heart, if that was the word, which was essentially cold, selfish and stupid.

She entered the cell, Parrish behind her, and said without ceremony, 'John Michael Murphy, are you prepared to sign the charge sheet and enter into your own recognizance to be bailed?'

He was not a man to answer a straight question straightforwardly, and took it as an excuse for pursuing his hobby of police-baiting.

'What's your name, miss? I will need it if I'm going to be lodging a complaint against me treatment here, and also over me arrest. I'm trying to remember whether I hit the constable first or he hit me – which, you see, would be police brutality.'

'My name's Inspector Darblay.'

'Ah, I thought it was. You're the one who's married to Tom Darblay, aren't you? And I've certainly heard about you, miss.'

Jean ignored the bait. 'Are you prepared to sign the charge sheet and be bailed? Yes or no?'

Still charmed by his own fantasies, he answered, 'If I said no, you'd just get your electric probes out. I'll sign it. I'll sign anything.'

'You've a court appearance on the fourteenth. Sergeant Parrish will write down the details for you.' She turned and went out. She had not liked the reference to Tom.

A message came through to her from Beck.

'I obtained entrance to nineteen Coleman Parade. There was a young girl inside, name Maeve Murphy, daughter of John Michael Murphy. She's been beaten up badly. She won't say it's her father did it, but I think he did. I've taken her down to Hartley General. A social worker at the hospital says the family is familiar to the Social Services. I put a quick call through to check.'

'Right, Sergeant. Get whoever deals with the Murphys to pick me up and come with me to the hospital.'

Tom was dealing with a lady who had problems with a missing husband and a missing pension-book when Jean's call came through to the Town Hall. It was taken by his Senior Officer, Jennie Randall, a brisk agreeable young woman with a tendency to look on the bright side. She found Tom's seniority in age to her comforting, and looked forward to involving him closely in cases. She listened carefully to what Jean had to say, and relayed it to Tom.

'Your wife's having a problem with the John Murphy family. She wants me to pick her up at the police station, to go to Hartley General. You'd better come along – you've met Murphy. I'm free now, if you are.'

'Yes, all right.' He dealt with the distressed lady, then drove Jennie to the station, where they collected Jean. On the way she told him something about the Murphy family, whom he had encountered with her once, at the beginning of his training period. He remembered the man having put up an eloquent plea for his own abandonment of his children to go on a two-day drinking bout. Jennie explained in detail to Jean, who had checked the records and discovered that Murphy figured frequently in them.

'Six months ago Murphy's wife, Margaret, died. That left him to bring up four children, all girls – age range five and a half to fifteen and a half.'

Jean forebore to ask what he was doing with four children if he was not prepared to behave responsibly to them; the answer was all too obvious.

'The original trouble,' Jennie went on, 'seems to stem from

his industrial accident, which led to a back problem. Since then he's only been able to do light work.'

'Such as fracturing jaws and breaking up pubs?' Jean hazarded. Tom shot her a surprised look.

'It's not easy,' Jennie said, 'for a man like that to respond to the death of a wife and suddenly get dumped with bringing up four kids.'

'Should be a sobering experience. At four a.m. this morning he was blind drunk, swinging his fists at Constable Farley. His back trouble seems to have improved.'

Jennie bridled. 'You don't understand, Inspector. Murphy's not very bright. He's got to raise these kids unaided. Of course he's going to turn to drink sometimes.'

'I shouldn't have thought there was any "of course" about it. A responsible man would control himself. From what I've seen of Murphy I should say the drink came first and the children a long way after. Anyway, this time it looks like he's beaten up his daughter, and that has to be my first concern.'

Jennie Randall looked as if she would like to say that this, too, was perfectly natural behaviour for a widower with back trouble, but she tightened her lips and said nothing. Tom looked from one to another of them. He was not used to hearing Jean at her hardest, on the warpath. It was an aspect of her that he knew existed, had seen before, but was not totally the Jean he knew . . .

Maeve Murphy was sitting up in bed, the livid marks on her face standing out against the white of the pillows. One covered the left side of her jaw, the other a cheekbone. She looked no more than a child, and a peaky sparrow-like child at that. She answered Jean's questions almost inaudibly. Yes, her ankle hurt badly. Yes, someone had kicked and hit her. But who it was she refused to say, staring dumbly back. At Jean's gentle request that the leg injuries should be revealed, the young Asian doctor uncovered the thin legs. One ankle was badly swollen, rainbow-coloured. Maeve winced when it was touched.

'A vicious beating,' the doctor said. 'Whoever did that meant to hurt.'

'Evidently. Will the facial bruises leave any permanent mark?'

'They should go in time.'

In time for the next lot, Jean thought. She sensed that Jennie Randall was impatient with the examination, already resolved in her own mind about the rights of the case.

Jean said, 'Goodbye, Maeve. Don't you think you'd better tell us who did this to you? If you don't we shall take it that it was your father.'

The only answer was a blank stare.

'If I can get her to admit it was him,' Jean said as they left the ward, 'I'm going to take action. I'll check out the other children. If I don't like what I see, I'll put a twenty-eight-day order on them.'

'Now wait a minute,' Jennie said sharply. 'Remember what I just told you, Inspector. This man is struggling to adjust to the death of his wife. He's not bright. That adjustment will involve things like getting drunk and lashing out. He's a man who happens to need a lot of constructive help.' Her large spectacles gleamed with challenge. Jean met it.

'You're saying that Murphy, who's beaten and kicked that child, is a poor unfortunate?'

'Not that exactly, but . . . And about Maeve, she's doing a terrific job – a real little substitute mother, feeding the kids, getting them up in the morning, getting them off to school. And you'd like to stop that with a quick twenty-eight-day order, get them put into the council-approved care home? They've lost their mother, now you want to tear them away from their dad?'

Tom was impressed by Jennie's fiery sincerity. In spite of the painful sight of Maeve, it convinced him that Jennie knew a lot more about the girl and her family than Jean did.

Jean came back at Jennie, her anger controlled. 'Murphy's beaten up his daughter,' she said. 'My reading is that he's a regular drunkard – that's what our records show – not a man who's suddenly taken to the bottle out of grief. He may shed crocodile tears about his late wife, but what sort of a life did she have with him? And has Maeve acquired that cowed look in just six months? Rubbish. He's done all this before and he'll do it again, and I have to do something about it. And the appropriate action to remove the possibility of his attacking his daughter again is an order to put the kids in care for a holding period of twenty-eight days while we sort him and the situation out.'

'Jean . . .' Tom began, but Jennie interrupted. 'You're not going to start the process of breaking up this family, Inspector, because I'm going to stop you.'

They were back at the Town Hall, Tom silent, Jennie still fuming.

'I'm going to talk to Murphy,' she said. 'I know where to find him at this time of day. Do you want to come with me?'

'Yes. Yes, I do.'

The Green Elm was a sleazy public-house in a run-down street which Jennie said was near Murphy's home. He was there, in a corner, sitting at a table, bowed over a pint of Guinness. They went over to him.

'Morning, John,' Jennie said. 'I've brought my assistant Tom Darblay along to see you.'

'Ah, Jennie me darling! Come and sit you down. What'll you take? Sure it's a pleasure to see you.' Tom was not fully aware how much the plain earnest Jennie was won over by the blarney with which Murphy addressed her, only that she smiled and softened and, much to Tom's surprise, accepted a drink, which Murphy paid for from a handful of money taken from what sounded like a very well filled pocket. Tom politely refused, but Murphy treated him like a long-lost friend nonetheless.

'Don't I remember when you came round to my home with this dear little girl here? Let it never be said John Murphy ever forgot a kind face or a kind word. I saw your wife this morning, Mr Darblay, and it's a mystery to me how a grand fella like you ended up married to that one – begging your pardon.'

There was no answer to this, but Jennie stepped in. 'Why did you hit Maeve last night, John?' she asked gravely. He laid a large hand on hers.

'You know, Jennie, and I swear it's the truth, I didn't remember about that until I got out of nick. I was walking down the road and suddenly the whole thing came back to me.' He groaned theatrically. 'Oh God . . . It was like this, you see. I usually go straight from the pub to me work – I go on shift nine o'clock at the bakery factory. Instead, I come home, found her – found my daughter Maeve, fifteen she is, in bed with a boy, some class of an Asian or Pakistani. I tried to grab him, but he run off like a shot rabbit.'

Jennie nodded encouragingly.

'Then I hit her. I shouldn't have. But I couldn't contain the anger sickening right up from my guts into my brain. I just saw red. Can you understand that, me darling?'

'I think you'd better talk to Maeve,' Jennie said gently.

'Sure, I'm going home at lunch. She'll be there feeding the kids.'

'She's in Hartley General,' Tom said. The man's face registered shock.

'Me little Maeve? Oh, what have I done to her?'

Jennie was watching Tom, letting him have his say in all this.

'You'd better go to her,' he said. 'Leave that drink and go there now.'

Murphy applied himself to the Guinness, as though reminded of it. He wouldn't be leaving much of it when he went. 'How can I face her, tell me that?' he demanded tragically. 'You know Maeve, Jennie. She's the one as keeps the whole bloody family together, begging your pardon, since Margaret went.'

'Jennie told me,' Tom said.

'You see, it was that little cocoa bastard in bed with her, and her only fifteen and a half. And because I couldn't get him, I turned on her.'

Jennie gave Tom an imperceptible nod. 'Come on,' he said, 'I'll take you to the hospital.'

'Sure, sure, that's very good of you.' Murphy took a long swig of his drink, draining the glass.

But when they reached the hospital they were told that Maeve had discharged herself.

'Ah, she'll have gone home. I'll go straight away.'

'You know the office number,' Tom said. 'Phone us as soon as you've talked to her.'

'I'll do that.' Murphy's tone was deep and sincere.

'And – stay off the drink!'

'Not a drop will I now touch. I swear it.'

Tom watched him go, oddly impressed. He had begun to take sides.

chapter twelve

John Murphy's resolution to stay off the drink lasted for at least ten minutes. The sitting-room of his shabby house in Salford Road was empty. He called Maeve's name, looked round the house, but there was no sign of her or of the three younger ones, Colleen, Maureen and Megan. For Maeve had been badly frightened by her father's attack on her, and had collected the children from school at the lunchtime break. As he searched the house, his four daughters were eating a scrappy picnic lunch in a bleak spot on the edge of the moor. They were cold and uncomfortable, but it was better than being at home.

'I won't be there when you come home this afternoon,' she told them. 'But I think I will come home when Da's at work, about midnight. Mind you wash your ears and clean your teeth before bed. And no fighting, mind.'

Murphy looked vaguely into the few rooms where his family might be supposed to be hiding, then went back into the sitting-room, straight to the object that had attracted his attention when he first went into it. Of course, a grand bottle of Scotch almost full. Just the thing to console a man deserted by his family. He had promised something to the fella from the Social, but that was in the emotion of the moment; he couldn't be expected to stick by it. He poured a very large drink, and swallowed it neat, then followed it with another. It seemed a pity to use up any more, with the rest of the day to get through. He went back to the Green Elm, where his friend Joxer Mulvany was already fairly drunk.

It didn't take Murphy long to get into the same state. The landlord gave them up to half an hour from closing time, then quietly but firmly told them they wouldn't be served with any more.

'I've got drink at home,' Murphy said. 'Let's go – maybe Maeve's there by now.'

Joxer brightened at the thought of a bit of shenanigan, and began to add fuel to his friend's smouldering temper. 'I'd like to go to your home,' he pronounced owlishly. 'I want to see you bow and scrape to the daughter for cloutin' her, because she was in the sheets with a little brown monkey.'

Murphy brooded. 'I shouldn't have hit her . . .'

'Thass right. You've got four kids to bring up, whassit matter if another little one comes along?' He watched gleefully the anger rise in Murphy, who got up, staggering.

'I've got to find that monkey and give him a pasting! You know, he's the one responsible for all of this!' It was the perfect solution, and a fine excuse for a bit of violence. Leaning on each other, the two left the pub.

Maeve was not at home. They collected the bottle of Scotch and went out to a different pub, where they bought another bottle. Then they walked waveringly through the streets to a patch of common land where, in a clump of bushes, they found a reasonable shelter from the wind in which they could drink undisturbed. With pauses for dozing they managed to make the bottles last until early evening.

'Pray tell me,' Joxer said, enunciating carefully, 'what we are doing sitting in this hedge?'

'Not for much longer. I know where that little gringo comes from, the one that was in the bed with Maeve. Over there he lives. That end street, number twenty-seven. And he works at Otley's. And he should be to his house about now. And I'm going to descend on him, mangle him, give him a Biblical pasting.' Murphy's voice became maudlin. 'I feel very bad, Joxer, very low. I've had about as much as I can take . . . I'm tired of it all, Joxer, and angry. I feel I have a right to fight back, Joxer, or go under. Because I feel I'm going under. Sinking. Sinking. Give me that bottle now . . .' He drained it.

The brown boy walking from the bus stop to the Murphys' front door smiled as he saw it open and Maeve emerge. She waved and came towards him. Neither of them saw the two lurking forms. Then Murphy's roar startled them, as he threw himself on the boy and began to maul him.

Maeve shrieked, 'Da, don't!' But he was too far gone in drunken rage to heed her. She flung herself at him and tried in her feeble way to drag him off the boy, scratching and pulling at him, drawing blood from his face. The boy saw his chance, wriggled out of Murphy's grasp and ran.

'You whore! You whore!' Murphy's bellow sent windows flying up and doors opening as he turned on the girl and pummelled her with his great fists until she collapsed on the pavement.

Jean sat in her Mini and watched as Beck and two ambulance men lifted Maeve into the ambulance. A neighbour had alerted the police; the street was full of interested spectators, watching as Jean joined Beck. Her expression was grim.

'So what about the other three kids?' she asked.

'A neighbour's looking after them, ma'am.'

'We'd better organize bringing them in. What happened to Murphy?'

'When last seen he was shooting off down the road.'

'Right, then. This time you and the lads *find* him! I'm going off watch. Phone me at home when you've got him.'

'Yes, ma'am.'

Tom and Jean had been to the hospital. Maeve was asleep, quite comfortable, the night nurse told them. Only her dark hair was visible, and her curled-up form looked very small . . .

They were quiet as Jean made their late-night coffee. There was a sense of strain between them, Jean's anger against Murphy and her determination to fix him had been strengthened by the sight of Maeve. Tom felt sympathy for the girl. But he couldn't help picturing the state of mind of the father who had gone against all fatherly feelings and attacked his child not once, but twice, driven on by incalculable emotional disturbance. He tried to tell Jean about it, or about his own rationalization of it.

'I don't know if I ever told you,' he said. 'When I was twelve or thirteen, my cousin and I were in the same class at St Augustine's. His mother died.'

Jean was looking unreceptive. 'Yes?'

'Well. His father, just after the death, moved the family out of their house and put it up for sale. My cousin, Joe, just couldn't accept his mum's death. He'd go round to the old house with its *For Sale* notice in the garden, and just hang around there. As if he was expecting his mother to appear somehow. As if he was trying to get comfort from the garden and the building where his mother had lived, and comforted and consoled him.' The message, Tom could see, was not getting home. 'Look, people who can't cope with a terrible reality resort to all sorts of things.'

'John Murphy resorted to whisky,' Jean said flatly, 'a lot of it, and very nasty he got with it. I'm not interested in your parallel between a little boy who's lost his mum and a grown man whose wife died after bearing him four kids and putting up with who knows what in the way of ill-treatment. D'you suppose the attacks on Maeve were the first he'd ever made on a woman?'

'There's nothing in the records about him assaulting his wife, is there?'

'No. She doesn't seem to have been the sort to complain. Bullies' wives don't, usually. Can we end this pointless conversation? Murphy beat up his daughter again, and that's my only concern. We have to take the appropriate steps.'

He flashed back at her, 'If the best you can do is trot out your standard police response, there's no discussion.'

'What does that mean?' Although she knew.

'You know what I bloody well mean. Your standard police response presumes there's some accepted standard of rational behaviour against which all infringements can be judged: "That woman is shoplifting, get her into a court." It doesn't matter that she's seventy and funny in the head because she's been living alone in one room for twenty years.'

'You think I'm as simple as that, then?'

They exchanged a look. 'You weren't simple when we met. I think you're changing. And it's got to be the job at Hartley.' He had said it, the thing that had been on his mind.

'You're wrong, you know.'

'I'm not asking for your opinion, I'm telling you mine. I

think seven years ago, when we were first married, you'd have understood Murphy, and not said, "He beats his daughter, that's my only concern, and the hell with him."

Jean held on to her patience. 'Over the years I've encountered a hundred Murphys. This happens to be *your* first six-foot-two-inch Paddy who has the power of the blarney but who fundamentally communicates with his fists.'

'You say it again in another line – you've encountered a hundred Murphys. That's what's happening to you, you find it easier to quantify people rather than qualify them: "He's one of a hundred Paddies." "She's a typical shoplifter." It's not right.'

Jean put down her cup in which the coffee had gone cold. The room was as familiar as ever, the room in which they drank their nightcaps and talked easily, relaxed, about the events in their day. Blackie slept on the rug, the light from a table-lamp showed the possessions they had chosen together, acquired together, the small treasures that had not after all been stolen from them. Yet everything was different, Tom turning against her after seven years of mutual tolerance and respect.

Carefully, choosing her words, she said, 'You've just criticized the effect of my job on me. I might just draw attention to the effect of yours on you, love. Once you'd have left this case to my experience, my judgement. Now you're bringing your own emotions into it. After just a few weeks, months, whatever, you think you know more about people like Murphy than I do, just because you're sorry for them.'

'I'm not just sorry – I understand the man!'

'Oh? How? Because you're both males? Is this a male solidarity front – you and Murphy, two of a kind? Do I take it that if I died in a crash or a shoot-out tomorrow you'd go on to the Scotch and start bashing people? Is that what you see as normal behaviour?'

Tom was alight with anger. 'Don't be ridiculous. And don't mock me. My feelings are sincere. Yours – they aren't even feelings, just parrot phrases.'

As angry herself, but cool, she said, 'I'm going to have Murphy's children taken into care – all four of them. He's attacked his daughter twice. Next time he might hit her with something other than his fists, maybe an iron bar. Then we'll be talking about something more serious than a twenty-eight-day order.'

'I'll see him through this. I'll sort him out. I'll stop him drinking, but leave him and his kids alone.'

'You and who else? God?'

'Laugh, go on. But I'm going to stop you doing this, Jean.'

'How?'

'In court.'

'*What?*'

'You expect to catch him tonight, don't you?'

'Yes. They're watching the bakery. If he doesn't turn up, and I shouldn't think he will, we'll get him somewhere else. He's too thick not to be caught. But when the case comes up on Friday you won't be in charge, Tom. You're still a junior officer, remember? Jennie Randall's the Social Services representative for that family, not you.' And I can handle her, Jean thought, she's soft-centred in a different way.

Tom said, levelly, 'Jennie's required at the post on Friday. She'll be one of the two officers on duty. She's handed over the court appearance to me, because I've worked on the case.'

There was a pause in which they looked at each other, and away, afraid of what they might see in each other's eyes. Then Jean said, 'Tom, I'm not going to have this. When you took that job there was always the chance of something like this happening. We didn't speak about it, we didn't have to. I'm a career policewoman. I can't have it happen. It's going to get to the local newspaper – husband social worker in court fight over problem family, with wife, Inspector Darblay of Hartley. And you know these things count in the Service.'

'Damn the Service. I'm more concerned with that family getting justice than how this might look to your superiors. Jennie agrees with me – she'd take just as strong a line if she were appearing. But she isn't and I am. It's fixed, there's nothing you can do about it.'

Jean got up and leaned on the mantelpiece, her face turned away from him.

'Well,' she said, 'this is the most God-awful thing that's happened in our marriage.'

'I agree.'

She made a last appeal. 'Do we have to behave like this?'

'Do *you*?'

'You're so positive I'm in the wrong.'

'Well, you are.'

'I'm not, Tom.' There was a moment when his conviction wavered for a moment. She had never lied to him, never pretended or put on official pomp to impress him. Somewhere he knew that the 'police responses' she had made to him were what she truly felt. If only he didn't feel so strongly about it himself . . .

She turned and abruptly left the room. He heard her go upstairs, and a few minutes later go out of the house. Her car started up; he knew that she had gone back to the station because she could no longer bear to be in the same house with him.

John Murphy turned up at Hartley General in the morning. Tom was there, ready to take Maeve to court when she was ready. He saw that Murphy was badly hung-over, apparently deeply upset. He heard him grovel to his daughter.

'I'm sorry, darling, terrible sorry. I will never do it again. Your da can't cope, Maeve. I drink and then I go mad, insane. Your father's promised to give up drinking now. I've said that many times during Mother's illness – and after. This time I mean it.'

The girl said nothing. She was dressed and cleaned up, the bruises still showing on her face, turning to fainter colours.

'Maeve, last night you were told you'd have to go to court, and the other children. I ask you this – you're sure that you want the home to be kept together – you and the kids and me?'

'Yes, Da!' She spoke flatly, as though reciting a creed.

The Juvenile Court was an unimpressive room, something of a glorified office. Three magistrates presided over it, two elderly men and one woman. Impassively they listened to Jean's request to apply for an order to commit the Murphy children into the care of the Local Authority for a period of twenty-eight days.

'Now, Inspector Darblay,' said the woman, 'we understand that your application is to be resisted by the Social Services Department present here?'

'Yes, ma'am.'

'Would the member of the Social Services identify himself or herself?'

Tom stood up. His name caused a ripple of reaction among the magistrates. They sensed a private conflict, and were not pleased. They listened to Jean's account of Murphy's two beatings-up of Maeve and to the contention of the Social Services Counsel that the second beating had not been serious. 'The girl was prescribed sedatives. The idea was that she would benefit greatly from a good night's sleep. Nothing more than that. As Inspector Darblay states, there is no contention that these two beatings took place, but we believe, as does Maeve Murphy, that whereas there was no complete excuse for John Murphy's behaviour, there were certain mitigating circumstances, and we'd like John Michael Murphy to take the stand.'

John Michael Murphy moved forward to the witness table and took the oath.

'My wife died four months ago,' he began. He stood straight, he was clear-eyed, all evidences of his hangover had vanished. He told the court, simply and eloquently, of the family's loss of income at his wife's death, of his struggle to keep the family together without relying on unemployment benefit. Questioned by Counsel, he freely admitted to being very drunk on the night he found Maeve in bed with the young Indian, and that he had been drunk again at the time of the second assault.

'I wonder how many in this court started working at eleven to keep a mam and da – Da being too past it to be working himself. Yes, I've worked a long life for pay packets, with never too much in them . . .'

Police Counsel interrupted. 'Mr Murphy, I'm not sure about the point that you're trying to make.'

'Just one minute, Mr Harmon,' said the lady magistrate. 'I for one think there's a great deal of relevance in what Mr Murphy is saying. Please continue, Mr Murphy.'

Murphy continued. His impassioned account of his own suffering, his poverty, his love for his children, held every ear. Jean whispered to Maggie Cullinane, 'He's a better actor than Laurence Olivier. We're going to lose.'

'There are men,' orated Murphy, 'in offices in London, Mayfair, who will tonight get into their big Daimlers and go home, open their cocktail cabinets, get drunk, hit the wife or girl friend, behind high walls. And no one will know. I am poor. And though I tell you honestly that I have been given to drink and I've a temper that leads to violence, yet after six months since my wife's death we still have a home intact, run by Maeve, and not destroyed by me.' He pointed dramatically to Jean and Maggie. 'And not, I ask you, to be destroyed by them. I will not ever go on the town again to get drunk. I will never raise my hand to Maeve again. I don't know what will be the outcome of this court, but whatever happens I'm telling you I've changed. The things I did to Maeve that brought me to here are the same things that have changed me. Please, do not break up my family . . .'

The magistrates adjourned. When they returned their spokeswoman announced that, having weighed all the circumstances, they had decided not to grant the twenty-eight-day application.

The parties concerned were close together in the narrow aisle after the magistrates filed out. Murphy said cheerfully to Jean, 'No hard feelings, Inspector.' She made no answer. Murphy moved to Tom, assured, confident that he had cut a good figure.

'Mr Darblay, what about joining us for a little drink?' he asked.

Tom stared, hardly believing his ears. When he spoke his voice was quiet but very angry. 'What the hell d'you mean? What have you just told the court? What did you tell Maeve this morning? That you'd give up drink.'

'Aw, come on, just the littlest dram – a tiny victory drink?'

'No.' Tom turned away sharply. Murphy's temper changed. 'All right! Have it your way.' He rounded on Maeve. 'You. Collect the kids, take them home.' She threw Tom a look – of pleading, perhaps, or simply telling him that this was how it was, would always be – then turned away, her thin shoulders hunched. Murphy strode out. At the Green Elm, Joxer would be waiting.

Jean had heard. Tom knew it. He came to her side.

'Well?' she said.

'We both lost.'

'Yes. It changes a lot.'

'What does it change?'

'I can't count on you a hundred per cent in the future.'

'Maybe that's a good thing,' he said. 'We have to be true to what we're sure is right. I think that's the thing that keeps a marriage together '

It nearly broke ours last night, she could have said. But there was no point. Tom had learned a lesson, painfully. Before long Murphy would be in trouble again, probably for something more serious than a beating-up. Tom would go on learning lessons, and they would go on differing. But she hoped, almost believed, that the fight they had just lost would turn into some kind of victory.

Further stories about the life and work of Inspector Jean Darblay will continue in *Juliet Bravo Two* by Mollie Hardwick to be published soon by Pan Books Ltd.